MYRIAM WARNER-VIEYRA was born in Guadeloupe, but has spent a large part of her life living in Senegal, where she has settled and raised her three children. She works at the University of Dakar as medical librarian in the Pediatrics Institute. Her Caribbean–African experience has given her valuable insights into the problems encountered in bridging the cultural differences of these two regions, and she draws upon her inside knowledge in painting such a sympathetic portrait of Juletane.

Her first novel *Le Quimboiseur l'avait dit* was published in 1980 and has been translated into English as *As the Sorcerer Said*. *Juletane*, written originally in French, is here made available in the English language through this translation by Betty Wilson, who lectures in French at the University of the West Indies, Jamaica, and is herself currently preparing an anthology of Caribbean women's writing.

MYRIAM WARNER-VIEYRA

JULETANE

Translated from the French by Betty Wilson

HEINEMANN

Heinemann Educational Books Ltd
22 Bedford Square, London WC1B 3HH

Heinemann Educational Books (Nigeria) Ltd
PMB 5205, Ibadan
Heinemann Educational Books (Kenya) Ltd
Kijabe Street, PO Box 45314, Nairobi
Heinemann Educational Boleswa
PO Box 10103, Village Post Office, Gaborone, Botswana
Heinemann Educational Books Inc.
70 Court Street, Portsmouth, New Hampshire, 03801, USA
Heinemann Educational Books (Caribbean) Ltd
175 Mountain View Avenue, Kingston 6, Jamaica

EDINBURGH   MELBOURNE   AUCKLAND
SINGAPORE   KUALA LUMPUR   NEW DELHI

First published by Heinemann Educational Books Ltd
in the Caribbean Writers Series in 1987

British Library Cataloguing in Publication Data

Warner-Vieyra, Myriam
Juletane.—(Caribbean writers series).
I. Title   II. Series
843 [F]   PQ3949.2.W3

ISBN 0–435–98978–2
0–435–98979–0 Export

Printed in Great Britain by
Richard Clay Ltd, Bungay, Suffolk

INTRODUCTION

The author

Myriam Warner-Vieyra is a Guadeloupean who has lived for many years in Senegal. Her first novel, *As the Sorcerer Said* (Longman, 1982) is set in Guadeloupe and Paris. *Juletane*, her second novel, a short companion volume to the first work, is set mainly in West Africa and in a sense might be considered by some to be an 'African' novel. Vieyra's writing is said to belong to both Caribbean and African literature. In a very real way, her works represent the links and continuities between the two as well as bearing witness to the connections, hidden and explicit, in a wider female literary tradition. Yet while Vieyra's themes and setting in *Juletane* might seem to be primarily concerned with an African reality, her sensibility remains essentially West Indian, more precisely, French Caribbean.

Caribbean women's writing in general

Until relatively recently, French Caribbean women's writing has been largely neglected. Yet it is an important and rich body of literature. Prose works by women from the francophone Caribbean appeared before the end of the nineteenth century, perhaps even earlier. The earliest writers were probably *creoles* (that is, white Europeans born in the West Indies), but the women whose works now form the major part of this literature are all *femmes de couleur* (women of colour). All would be considered 'black' in the European or North American context, but in the fine distinctions of their own societies they range, like the heroines of their novels, over a wide and complexly designated colour spectrum. The variety and number of terms which exist to distinguish between skin shades or colour types in their society suggest that the matter of colour is one which is central in French Caribbean colonial and post-colonial contexts. This preoccupation is evident in the literature: colour is a dominant theme. Often it is linked to class divisions. Earlier Caribbean writers in particular seem excessively concerned, even obsessed, with matters of race and colour.[1] Perhaps the explanation lies in the nature of the reality out of which the literature springs. The literature of the Caribbean, perhaps more so than most, is intimately linked to its historical and social contexts with their values and ambiguities.

Most writers who grew up in the French-speaking Caribbean were first educated in local 'French' schools and then in many instances at universities in France. Some of them lived and travelled widely in France and West Africa. Many spent the greater part of their adult lives outside the West Indies. During the colonial period there was a constant movement of the educated black population between the Caribbean, France and French African territories. This movement largely continued until the independence of the former French African territories in the 1960s. Many of the women from the West Indies found themselves in West Africa via the *metropole* either as teachers, civil servants or wives of French Africans, often fellow students encountered in France. Among contemporary writers, a greater number are originally from Guadeloupe than from Martinique. This is not true of male writers – a detail perhaps not without significance. Guadeloupe is generally seen as more militantly nationalistic and as leaning more towards independence, while Martinican society with a larger European, white, population is still largely directed towards metropolitan France. Many of these French Caribbean writers were, at one time or another, actively involved with women's organizations and groups concerned with reform in the role and status of women.[2] The works of francophone Caribbean women therefore reflect the ways in which many women, especially educated coloured women, see or saw themselves in their society. It is a literature of confinement and alienation rather than a literature of revolt.

Caribbean women's writing up to the present cannot be said to be militantly 'feminist': generally it does not depict, openly advocate, or point to the possibility of a change in the status or situation of women, which is seen mainly as negative.[3] However, the preoccupations of the writing point to the necessity for change and are '*feminist*' in the wider sense of having to do primarily with women's lives. The works speak of the feminine condition. They make a significant contribution, especially with regard to the position and image of the educated woman. In general, the picture that emerges is pessimistic.

In many works the female first person narrative predominates. Often the narrator makes explicit that the reason for and the act of writing gives consolation, relief, or simply a sense of coming to terms and attempting to cope with a reality which has become, or is becoming, increasingly intolerable. 'I had chosen a wide, flower-filled road and it had become transformed into a narrow path full of ambushes; but I could not turn back, there was no other way open to me...' remarks Zetou, the tragic heroine of Myriam Warner-Vieyra's first novel, *As the Sorcerer Said*. Her statement sums up the experience and the fate of many another Antillean heroine. The women in these works are haunted by a deep sense of failure, of dislocation and alienation. In Simone Schwarz-Bart's imagery they are little fish who have lost their 'nageoires' – the stabilizing element which enables them to stay upright and afloat in the currents of the vast ocean or river of life, they are like 'baleines échouées', lost whales washed up on the beach.[4]

The narrative structure mirrors the state of mind and predicament of the protagonist/narrator. The autobiographical first person narrative is particularly suited to the woman's introspective journey. The themes in the novels often have to do with this tragic situation which, on the personal level, is marked by frustration, ambivalence, ambiguity, self-hatred, feelings of rejection and of the impossibility of reconciling conflicting parts of the self. It is an identity crisis, or 'quest' common to male West Indian writing, anglophone and francophone alike, but perhaps even more acute in the case of the French Caribbean woman who is *assimilée*.[5] Unlike in male Caribbean fiction and anglophone women's writing, however, this crisis usually ends in withdrawal and/or flight/evasion rather than confrontation and breaking out. The heroines flee to France, Africa, or withdraw from external reality. Through the fields of action of the novels, the three geographical and psychological spaces – Africa, France, the Caribbean – are explored in terms of a personal history. The result in most cases is alienation and rejection.

Many of the other features which characterize women's fiction in the Caribbean are also linked to the autobiographical form. The focus is, naturally, on the woman. The works are marked by their pessimism which extends not only to the condition of woman but also to that of the male and to their view of Caribbean and neo-colonial African society in general. This negative view results in and is caused by a feeling of alienation. The women are alienated from themselves, from men and from their society.

Their alienation is linked to feelings of rejection and expresses itself in negative mother and father figures: a rejection both of natural parents and of the past. This rejection of their history is expressed as disillusionment with the island-mother, with Europe, the mother or fatherland (*la mère-patrie*), as well as disappointment with Africa, the mythical motherland. The women's alienation and feelings of rejection lead them to try to find ways of escape but they find there is no real escape, only withdrawal from reality which in turn leads to a longing for death, suicide, or madness. The women often see themselves as victims: victims of a hostile environment and victims of their history and heritage. The past is linked to their identity and their alienation is often seen as a result of historical factors – family history and the history of their society. Thus Juletane attributes her misfortunes in part to the circumstances of her birth, or rather her conception, as well as the weight of centuries of oppression which her frail shoulders are forced to bear. In later novels the women have consciously rejected their society's distorted sense of hierarchy based on colour and sex but have been conditioned to internalize these values, and they find they cannot simply discard them. Zetou, the protagonist of Vieyra's *As The Sourcerer Said*, declares that if, like her sister, just as intelligent, but less ambitious, she had been content to stay in her tiny native village, her story would have had a happy, rather than a tragic ending. The novel carries a warning in the form of a cautionary epigraph: 'Where confidence leads you, your strength cannot save you (Antillean proverb)'. It is a theme, among others, which Vieyra picks up again and examines in *Juletane*.

The text

On the surface *Juletane* is a simple novel. It is the story of a Western woman of colour, in this case a French West Indian, who meets and marries an African in Europe and then finds she cannot fit in to his traditional African family, especially as she has to share her husband with two co-wives. It is a story about alienation, madness, shattered dreams: the disillusioned West Indian outsider's disenchantment with Africa – all familiar themes in Caribbean fiction. It is also a novel about polygamy – a subject which has been treated before in African women's writing. (It is a theme for example of Mariama Bâ's poignant *So Long a Letter* (Heinemann, 1981).) What makes Vieyra's novel different is the subtle and complex treatment of these familiar themes. It is full of gentle ironies. Juletane, the West Indian, who prides herself on her independence, proves to be as dependent as Awa, the traditional 'uneducated' wife. In fact, more so. Juletane's story is also a compelling narrative. The reader is carried along with Helene, the other protagonist in this double narrative, caught up in Juletane's whirlpool. Vieyra does not take sides. She looks at four women's lives, at the paths they have taken, at the possibilities open to women in the Caribbean, in Africa, in life. She forces the reader, through Juletane and Helene, to re-examine easy assumptions, to look again at safe generalisations.

It is Juletane's story, but through the pretext of the diary Vieyra examines the roles and dreams of these four women, two African, two Caribbean, and manages to raise many issues, touch many chords. The novel has 'feminist' preoccupations. Juletane is the confused, sheltered Caribbean woman who needs to 'find herself' and her place in the world, who invests too much in her relationship with the man in her life to the detriment of her own self. Helene is at the opposite extreme: a self-reliant career woman reluctantly about to become a wife. Their lives touched briefly but it is Juletane's diary which brings them together. The events in the novel take one night in the case of Helene's narrative, several months in Juletane's life. But for Helene the night's vigil is symbolic of an emotional journey, a cleansing and revitalizing ritual.

Helene finds Juletane's diary at a crucial moment in her life. She is about to marry. Her reasons are entirely selfish: she wants a child. The idea of adopting one of her many nieces and nephews does not really appeal to her. To fulfil her desire it must be a child of her own. So she allows herself to be persuaded by a young African to become his wife. Ousmane, her fiance, is completely fascinated by Helene.

She is unlike any woman he has met before: independent, decisive, totally in control of her life. Or so it seems. He is delighted when she agrees to marry him. But Helene has only consented because she thinks by marrying Ousmane she is risking nothing.

Moving from the cramped studio apartment she has occupied for ten years, however, is symbolic of the change Helene is unwittingly about to make in her deliberately restricted life. Her new spacious apartment has a garden. She will share it with Ousmane. But Helene does not intend to share her life in any real way or to relinquish control. She has calculated exactly what she has to gain or lose from the move. It is a transaction, carefully planned, which she sees as to her advantage. (She has even had a marriage contract prepared, detailing what property she is deeding to her husband-to-be. She sets her own bride price!) Helene's attitude to Ousmane is indulgent and patronizing. By marrying him she imagines she will retain the control and independence she has always enjoyed. She will not be vulnerable. But vulnerability, and remaining vulnerable, are necessary conditions for any relationship. If Helene will not take this risk, in her new situation she will remain dissatisfied and unfulfilled, as she secretly admits she has been for years.

Juletane's diary forces her to confront herself and to deal with feelings and questions she has been suppressing or evading for a long time. In the novel the two narratives alternate in a contrapuntal relationship. The events and circumstances of her young compatriot's story seem to comment on Helene's life and she is struck by the contrasts.

Juletane's vulnerability, her spontaneous naivety, sharply contrast with Helene's sensitive self-protectiveness, her total dependence with Helene's fiercely independent nature. Juletane is trusting, affectionate, open. She holds back nothing. When her husband betrays her trust, Juletane is devastated. Like a wounded animal, she strikes back, in a frenzy, and her wounded pride becomes destructive as she lucidly defends her innocence. Juletane is overwhelmed by circumstances, which seem to conspire against her. Helene's normal posture is to remain aloof. Reading the diary is cathartic for her. It is the medium by which all the self-imposed, protective layers are gradually stripped away in the course of the night when she reads Juletane's story, straight through, without being able to put it down.

Juletane's diary, she says, is addressed to her husband, who never has the chance to read it. But more importantly it serves to define for Juletane herself, as for Helene, the path her life has taken. Writing it gives her the possibility to exert a control and an ability to shape, direct and understand, which have hitherto eluded her. The complex narrative structure links her to the reader through Helene. Vieyra's narrative is an imaginative feat. She describes the relentless logic of Juletane's increasingly wandering mind as she loses touch with 'reality'. Vieyra also questions the nature of that 'reality' as she questions the nature of 'madness'.

> 'What if mad people weren't mad? What if certain types of behaviour which simple, ordinary people call madness, were just wisdom, a reflection of the clearsighted hyper-sensitivity of a pure, upright soul plunged into a real or imaginary affective void?

Juletane pleads for an alternate vision, a re-vision.

In French Caribbean fiction so far the sensibility of the French West Indian woman is one which is given to self-doubt, to self-dramatization, to 'quitting' rather than coping. (Simone Schwarz-Bart's stalwart, mythical heroines are the exemplary exceptions.) Confronted with the abyss, those women do not seem to have the power to resist the void.[6] But in *Juletane* an important new step is taken. A dimension is explored and a link is forged. Juletane's story, unlike Zetou's in Vieyra's first novel, impacts on her fellow-countrywoman and, perhaps, changes her life. The diary creates an emotional bond with Helene and restores Helene's capacity to feel. It gives her life. All Juletane's acts except her writing are destructive and self-destructive. Significantly she takes no responsibility for them. While she is clearly their author, she refuses to acknowledge herself as such. This is not the case with her diary. She creates herself, and she re-creates Helene as she writes her story. Writing enables her to strike out at the West Indian fatalism which makes her feel she has no control over her destiny, decided at birth by her history.

The prevalence of autobiographical fiction in Caribbean women's literature has already been mentioned. This is also true of African women's writing and of women's writing in general. That is not to say that the works are necessarily autobiographical. (There is no evidence to suggest that Juletane's story in any way parallels Miriam Warner-Vieyra's life.) Except that both are West Indian women living in a West African society, there seem to be few similarities: Vieyra has been married for many years to Paulin Vieyra, a well-known film critic and they have three children, to whom the novel is dedicated. It is simply that the structure of the fictional autobiography, journal, diary, letter or other related 'intimate' genres seems to be the preferred vehicle for expressing feminine/feminist/female consciousness. The autobiographical form allows a sort of re-vision, a radical re-shaping of a life, seen and recounted from the inside, which fits in with a 'problematic' protagonist's attempts to define and order reality.

In *Juletane* Vieyra uses this form and expands and complicates it to create contrasting, often ironic, portraits which serve as a vehicle for reflecting on women's roles and aspirations. Minor characters like Helene's sisters in the West Indies, and more importantly Juletane's co-wives, function in this way. Awa, Mamadou's first wife, is the traditional mother-figure while Ndeye, the grasping, materialistic 'modern' third wife is portrayed as the whore.

Awa defines herself solely in terms of her relationship with her/their husband. Hers is a somewhat stereotyped portrait of the 'traditional' African wife: 'uneducated', gentle, submissive, self-effacing to a fault. Juletane, the outsider, depicted as the 'mad woman', the 'barren tree', attributes these attitudes to Awa's upbringing. She comments that for Awa 'the universe is confined to a mat under a tree and her three children around her'. Yet Juletane also appreciates her co-wife's qualities: her refinement, her generosity, her tact and restraint. Her sense of justice is outraged that their husband relegates Awa to the kitchen and will only be seen in public with his vulgar, glamorous third wife because she has a veneer of Western 'education'.

Vieyra's portraits of these minor characters at times seem to be too broadly sketched to be realistic, but the concerns she is addressing are clear. The women's relationship to each other and to themselves is mediated exclusively through the man they share in common. They are 'co-wives' and they do not relate to each other except to vie for the favours of the man or to accept their allotted portion. Ndeye, the one who manoeuvres most cunningly, gets the greatest share. The household is dominated by the presence and patronage of the male. There is no female bonding; no strong ties exist between the women as women, as friends, outside the male-centred relationship. When Juletane opts out of this she cuts herself off from any possibility of integrating within the household or outside it. Yet her desire for affection and sympathy from the other women remains. It is expressed explicitly in passing allusions to Awa's kindness and gentleness towards her, in the reference to the look of silent compassion which she thinks she reads in the eyes of her cruel co-wife's female companion, Binta. Through the medium of her diary Juletane not only reaches out to her husband but also touches Helene, her superficially tough but soft-hearted compatriot. The importance of Vieyra's novel is that it describes sensitively and powerfully a reality that is intimately known to the author and raises critically issues which are relevant not only in Africa and the Caribbean but in the wider context of human relationships.

Notes

1 See for example Mayotte Capécia's *La négresse blanche* ('The white negress', Corréa, Paris, 1950) and Michèle Lacrosil's two novels, *Sapotille* (Gallimard, Paris, 1960) and *Cajou* (Gallimard, Paris, 1961). The heroines of all three novels are obsessed with their colour.

2 Jacqueline Manicom (*Mon examen de blanc*, Sarrazin, Paris 1972) was co-founder of the French women's group 'Choisir' and was active in the Women's Movement in France.

3 Manicom's works and those of Simone Schwarz-Bart are perhaps notable exceptions.

4 Simone Schwarz-Bart, *The Bridge of Beyond* (Heinemann, London, 1982) p. 30.

5 'assimilée': that is assimilated to/by French, European values, education, culture.

6 Compare the attitude of Antiguan writer Jamaica Kincaid's Woman, more typical of protagonists in anglophone Caribbean women's writing, who declares: 'I said I don't want to fall any more and I reversed myself. I was standing again on the edge of the deep hole. I looked at the deep hole and I said, You can close up now, and it did' (*At the Bottom of the River*, Pan Books, London, 1984, p. 42) with Vieyra's Zetou (*As the Sourcerer Said...* Longman, London, 1982, p. 78) who says: 'Once more I could feel myself slipping down into a chasm. This time I made no attempt to halt my descent into the valley of darkness'.

BETTY WILSON
University of the West Indies, Mona, Kingston, Jamaica.

African terms italicised in the text can
be found in the glossary on page 83.

To the three men in my life
Paulin, Nanou, Stephane.

To my daughter Celia, whose mathematical
interests are so far removed from my wandering
pen.

Nothing is farther from what one dreams of than a husband

BARONNE GARAT

JULETANE

They say a removal is as bad as a fire. That's not quite true. After a removal you can prune, choose to keep or throw out, uncover long forgotten objects, which may prove to be much more interesting than they seemed years before. After a fire, what is left in the ashes is almost never of any use.

Those were the thoughts which no doubt ran through Helene Parpin's mind. Helene Parpin, very much her own woman, who, until that Friday afternoon in February, ordered her life as she saw fit, giving priority to 'me first'.

That day, Helene was sorting her things in preparation for the move from the studio which she had occupied for ten years to her new spacious apartment. She had recently decided to get married, for the simple reason that she wanted a child of her own. She was fond of her husband-to-be. He was ten years her junior, a handsome athletic man, six feet tall, eighty kilos, gentle as a lamb. She was his superior financially and intellectually. Too independent by nature, she could not have tolerated a husband who would dominate her, make the decisions, take the lead.

A green, cardboard folder, bleached by time and the sun, slid out from a pile of books she was about to stack in a box already half-full. She picked up the folder. It had nothing written on it and she had no recollection of its contents. Helene sat down to rest a few minutes and opened the cover. Mechanically, she leafed through an old dog-eared, exercise book and the few odd sheets of paper which were in it, then she began to read.

The document, covered with an irregular handwriting in black crayon, was in the form of a diary.

1

Tuesday, August 22, 1961, 4.00 p.m.

Born one twenty-fifth of December, a day of rejoicing, in a small village on a little island in the Caribbean, I was, by virtue of this fact, conceived one night in Lent, a period of fast and abstinence. Contrary to popular belief, which attributes a definite ascendancy to the signs of the zodiac prevailing at the time of one's birth, in my case, it was the date of conception which must have influenced my personality traits and the course of my life. My father, in paying homage to his young wife, had flouted tradition, and begot me with all the condemnation of the village church. At birth, then, I was already a victim of the elements, not to mention three centuries of our people's history which my frail shoulders were to inherit ...

The idea of writing came to me this morning as I was distractedly thumbing through a half-used exercise book which had fallen out of a school bag. The exercise book belonged to a little girl who might have been my daughter, my child. Alas! I have no children. I have no parents, no friends. Not even a name any more. But that is not important, it was only a borrowed name and I fear I have forgotten it. My real name I have never known, it was erased from the register of time.

Here, they call me 'the mad woman', not very original. What do they know about madness? What if mad people weren't mad! What if certain types of behaviour which simple, ordinary people call madness, were just wisdom, a reflection of the clear-sighted hypersensitivity of a pure, upright soul plunged into a real or imaginary affective void?

To me, I am the most lucid person in the house. Even though on certain bitter days, I am filled with rage when I hear Ndeye boasting about our husband's prowess in bed. She is so spiteful!

Here she is again today today, with her friend Binta, in the courtyard, right under my window, and to make sure that I don't miss a single word of their conversation they are speaking French.

2

'My dear Binta, Mamadou is extraordinary, not at all like those men who take their pleasure and leave you unfulfilled. He is even sensitive enough to make sure I am really satisfied ...'

And then Binta who has all the appearances of a frustrated woman is seized with a paroxysm of false laughter, full of hypocritical 'ha! ha! has!'. I open my shutters abruptly. One of them knocks off Binta's wig, freezing her laughter into an exclamation of astonishment and exposing her dull, dirty hair rolled up in little patches which have not seen a comb for several months. Ndeye seizes the opportunity to give vent to her usual volley of abuse directed at me. Binta shamelessly replaces the tangled black mane which she wears on her head for hair. Everything about her betokens careless neglect. Her nails, long and dirty, are covered with chipped nail polish, as vivid as the black dirt that shows through beneath. Her shoes are stained with grease: from in front jut toes whose ingrown nails have traces of varnish which once must have been the same colour as the polish on her fingers; from behind protrude heels cracked like the earth in the dry season. Her shiny *boubou* and her jewellery would have been more suited to an evening out. Although she is too fat, she has a lovely face with regular features and a gentle look. From her mouth she takes her *soccu* which she had been rubbing idly against her already clean teeth, and spits a long stream of saliva through the space in her incisors. She feels sorry for me. You can see it in her eyes: they are filled with compassion.

She smiles at me. At least I think she does.

Caught up in the story and as if spellbound, Helene settled herself comfortably in an armchair to continue reading. Midnight. Sleep would wait. Why hadn't she felt any curiosity to read the diary before? What unforgiveable negligence! A very bad habit acquired some time before: she always put off reading anything she thought might be boring. Thus she had totally forgotten this notebook. When they had given it to her, she'd thought it a completely disjointed tale, incoherent ramblings. After two pages, she saw that the story interested her and that she was eager to read it right through. Once again, she had been a victim of her prejudices.

I am going to have to change, to learn to trust others, especially my future husband, Helene thought. She scratched her head, took out a hairpin which had been sticking in her scalp then went back to reading her story.

Ndeye is foaming with rage. She continues to gesture in my direction, jangling her numerous gold bracelets, one of the many reasons for the chronic shortage of money we have been suffering for the past two years.

The hatred she feels for me is evident, but inexplicable ... I watch her, without understanding what she is saying, too preoccupied with my own thoughts. She is not as pretty as her companion, with a flat nose and a mouth that is too big, but she takes more care of her appearance, her braids are regularly redone, every day she takes endless baths with all sorts of dubious ingredients acquired from the *marabout* and aimed at keeping our husband permanently in her bed. Not to mention all the perfumes from east and west which she blends into the *cuuraay* that she uses for her room and her clothes. Her nail polish scarcely has a chance to chip, for even the glass of water to quench her thirst has to be brought to her. She does not hesitate to call the maid, ask her for water, even though she is just sitting there idle or doing nothing better than looking at her corpulent body sprawled on her bed, or overflowing in a chair. When she does go into the kitchen, it is to prepare a special dish for Mamadou's evening meal, on a gas stove, while the midday rice, cooked on a charcoal fire, is left exclusively to Awa, the first wife, or to the young woman who works for the household.

Awa, a little way off, is sitting on a mat, under the mango

tree in our yard. She is playing with her three children, bouncing Oulimata, the youngest girl, up and down. She is smiling, apparently unaware of what is going on between Ndeye and me. She never interferes in what does not concern her directly. As far as she is concerned, the whole universe stops at a mat under a tree and her three children around her.

It is hot and humid, awful. You can feel a storm in the air. I close my shutters gently, in response to Ndeye's wrath and find myself once more in the pleasant half-light of my room.

My bed: a cheap iron box-spring; for a mattress, a pallet which I keep vainly turning day after day, and which in spite of this, never loses the shape of my body, forcing me to be exactly in the middle, in the hollow formed by the strained springs. Next to the bed, two empty whisky crates serve as my bedside table. To the left of my bed, a small chest which holds my treasures, more of sentimental than any real value. I hope that they won't take it away from me, like the table Mamadou unceremoniously took to replace the one in the kitchen which termites had eaten ...

I snitched an exercise book belonging to Diary, Awa's eldest daughter. It was the only way I could have something to help me record my thoughts. Only two pages had been used. Writing will shorten my long hours of discouragement, will be something for me to cling to and will give me a friend, a confidante, at least I hope it will ...

How ever did I fall into this well of misery, where my body has been lying for years, while my rebellious soul wears itself out in useless attempts to revolt, which leave me even more broken, more defeated than ever? I think I have tried to get out; my fingertips still remember the smooth clay of the walls which my hands reduced to powder, grasping for something solid to cling to, until I was drunk with exhaustion. It seems as if I found nothing and that with time I have become accustomed to living half a life.

It was before the well, four or five years ago perhaps. I

don't know anymore. I had met my husband, or rather our husband, Mamadou, one evening at a garden-party at the Cité Universitaire in Paris. I happened to be there more or less to please a friend. Unlike other girls of my age and from my country, I didn't like to dance and didn't know how. Not even the *beguine*, to the great dismay of all those for whom this 'divine dance' was life itself. Mamadou noticed. He thought me funny. 'A black woman who dances like a broomstick!'

'Tell me! Haven't you ever danced before?' he said with a wide, mocking grin.

'Does it bother you?' I replied, annoyed, shrugging my shoulders and deliberately turning my back on him. At this he took hold of my hands firmly.

'Now, don't sulk, come, I'll teach you to dance.' With Mamadou's guidance, I didn't do too badly. He danced with me two or three times. We parted without arranging to meet, not thinking we would see each other again.

Several days later, walking up the Boulevard Saint Michel, I became aware of someone beside me.

'Chance does arrange things,' said a voice. It was Mamadou.

'Hello, I didn't think I would see you again so soon,' I replied.

'I did.'

'Really?'

'Really. Let's go and have coffee to celebrate,' he said, pulling me along with him.

I could have refused; ordinarily because of my bourgeois up-bringing, I did not accept spur-of-the-moment invitations. Yet I gave in, because I had begun to like him already.

Mamadou was very tall, he had a small moustache, a quick and easy smile, white, even, teeth, lively, mischievous eyes. His free and easy manner, far from shocking me, amused me. One would have thought he was seeing me for the first time. He examined me shamelessly from head to toe. My friends thought me pretty, perhaps I was. I had no idea.

6

I hoped that Mamadou's careful scrutiny would be positive. I had a finely chiselled, oval face, a well proportioned body for my medium height. My long, thick hair was neither frizzy nor too curly. I wore my hair in braids, one on either side of my head, coiled over my ears. According to certain people, this hairdo made me look like the type of *ingénue* who hardly exists anymore these days.

I was an *ingénue*, an ignorant and foolish girl, brought up by her godmother, a strict, devout, old maid. Since her death, a year before, I had been discovering the world. That July I had exchanged my dark, severe clothes for little summer dresses, light and low-cut. All the same, I still did not dare to change my hairdo and especially not to cut my hair, which would have been a real sacrilege. My godmother would have been capable of coming to pull me by the feet, at night. She had threatened me with that when she was alive. Since I knew nothing about the power of the dead, I preferred not to provoke their anger. So, I was satisfied just to admire the latest styles: short hair and permanents.

After the coffee in the 'Select', Mamadou invited me to dinner for the following evening. The hours in between were so long … I saw the little room that I occupied on the sixth floor of an old fashioned building in the area near Les Halles for the first time in all its ugliness. Summer, dry, hot, with a marvellous sun, danced in the streets. My room, on the other hand, remained damp, dark, heavy with boredom.

I opened the fanlight which served as a window. It went right up to the roof. I could see only the sky, the grey wall stained with damp green blotches, and the slant of the slate roof of the next building. Here and there the uniform colour of the slate was broken by a red brick chimney. I was really alone, I had nowhere to go to exchange ideas, simple pleasantries, which fill up the time. All my friends had left Paris for the holidays. As for me, I was too 'stone broke' after buying my summer dresses; and I also had to think about a new coat for the winter. I went to bed quickly, without eating, to shorten the hours and to dream of the next day's dinner with Mamadou.

It is too dark to keep on writing. I open my shutters again, softly. Binta, her wig and her friend Ndeye have gone back into the drawing-room. They are saying goodbye now, each sending regards to the other's husband. The little servant girl is sweeping the yard for the tenth time. The moment she seems to be having the slightest bit of rest, if there is nothing else to be done, Ndeye asks her to sweep up the yard. No sooner has she finished, than it seems everyone takes pleasure in dirtying it again. The children are teasing each other on the mat spread out under the mango tree, waiting for dinner time. Awa is in the kitchen. You would think she is fighting with the pots: they are banging against each other in a deafening clatter. The children, the young servant girl, Awa and I were often the only ones around the 'bowl' at the evening meal. Ndeye would wait for Mamadou who came home very late; she prepared delicacies for him, which he usually enjoyed in her company. Sometimes, there would be guests. Awa would help Ndeye but always stayed in the kitchen, without taking part in the festivities. This situation did not seem to bother her. She took Mamadou into her bed, whenever Ndeye allowed it, and gave him children. What did she get in rturn? A few *pagnes*, a little food, very few jewels compared to the treasures which Ndeye had. Yet she deserved much more consideration from her husband. She had given him children who were his pride, she was refined, pretty, and of a discretion which I could not help admiring, in spite of everything.

It is going to be dark soon. I have no idea what time it is and I am not hungry ... I am going to have a shower and go to bed. I can't do anything else, because the light bulb in my room is burnt out. To change it, I will have to wait for the end of the month, the master's salary and his goodwill. There is a storm in the air, if only it would rain.

8

Wednesday, August 23, 1961, 7.00 a.m.

I open my shutters to the cool of a fleecy blue sky in the rainy season. The rain and the storm have soothed my long sleepless night, peopled with confused images of a former time when I was full of hope. Then, I used to love those long, late, nights, for sleep and dream would blend harmoniously into dawn. For years now, my mornings, a succession of long monotonous hours, have stretched out interminably. Today, however, I feel, I breath, I am alive. A prayer comes to my mind: 'Thank you, Lord, for this new day, when I feel born again, from the bottom of my depths of solitude. I cry to you. Show me, I pray, the path of true liberty. Give peace to my soul. Teach me to forgive them, make me an example of wisdom for this house. You have said, and I believe, that your wisdom is folly for men.'

The courtyard is deserted again for the moment, waiting for Awa to appear. The clothes left on the line have been scattered by the wind and form little piles of damp colour. The only tree, a bushy mango, bare of fruit, with brilliant foliage stretches its shade over our daily chores. I tidy my room, turn my mattress, shake out my sheets, crush a cockroach, sweep. I am overflowing with life and energy; once more I pick up my notebook and the thread of my memories, while the household gradually stirs.

We had dinner in a Chinese restaurant in the Boulevard Montparnasse, then Mamadou and I went to the cinema. I would have liked to have seen one of the latest popular films; the billboards, in fact, displayed a giant Martine Carole with ample bosoms, or Gerard Philipe my idol. Mamadou did not ask me to choose. A masterpiece of the seventh Japanese art was showing in a little neighbourhood cinema and he absolutely had to see it. I have never understood what the film was about. The room was full, I couldn't read the subtitles. I was bored to death.

9

Later on, rather than dark movie theatres, I preferred to stroll along the 'Boule-Miche' or to chat with friends in a café. Sometimes on a Sunday we would spend the day with a couple, student friends of ours, at their house, where we met other friends. The conversation always revolved around the same subject, of prime importance: the future of Africa, independence. Some of them formulated bold plans, formed governments, assigned themselves ministerial portfolios, or an ambassadorship, preferably in Paris. A tiny minority, really just one man, thought that independence would be the ruin of Africa, would increase tribalism and that the best solution would be control of their own resources within the framework of French laws and institutions. This was all too much theory for me. I knew nothing about my own homeland ... At ten after my father's death, I had left my island to go and live in Paris with my godmother who took her role very seriously. Despite her meagre resources, she tried hard to give me the kind of education which she thought would be worthy of my father's daughter. 'He was a wonderful man', she would say. He was perfect.

My father, twenty years older than my mother, had married her after being a widower for many years. His first wife was one of Godmother's sisters. She had been swept away by a tidal wave, during a hurricane, clutching her two children in her arms. My godmother escaped, minus one buttock, sliced off by a sheet of zinc. I still wonder how the zinc's aim could have been so accurate ...

Godmother was quieter than my mother. My mother was beautiful, young. She died at nineteen, right after I was born. My maternal grandmother took care of me until my father's death, several years later, when I was sent to France. My godmother's wish was to fulfill the obligations she had undertaken on the day of my baptism. From then on I was almost completely cut off from my island home and from other young people my age.

Apart from going to school, I never went out, except with

my godmother, most of the time to visit her friends, women who were all over fifty. Once or twice a year, we went to a live concert. *Pas-de-loup* concerts.* Godmother said that music was the most beautiful thing in the world. It was the only thing which could lift the soul to the untouched heights of the real joy of living. She wanted me to learn to play the violin. Unfortunately I hated the teacher she chose, an old concert artiste, decadent and slovenly. So, with a lot of tact, I managed to convince her that I preferred to remain the type of music lover who enjoys the art by listening to others play. On Sunday evenings we listened to broadcasts of philharmonic orchestra concerts from different European capitals.

We lived in a small flat in Paris, two rooms and a kitchen. My godmother had spent her whole life working in a local tailoring establishment, which made custom-made suits. My dresses, which she made, had the same severity as the tailored suits she sewed all day long. Apart from music, all we talked about was the fashion world and its little bits of gossip. Having passed my *brevet*, a few days after I had started my first job I came home to find Godmother was not there. She was hardly ever late; she always arrived home at five-thirty, doing her errands on the way. I waited half an hour then set out to meet her. I walked two kilometres all the way to the work-room which closed at four-thirty. I retraced my steps calling at the bakery and the butcher's where she generally shopped. No one had seen her that evening. I was seized with a sudden anguish. I suddenly felt all alone in a hostile world. I ran all the way home and rushed up the six flights of stairs. Her absence weighed heavily on me; I went back down to the concierge's flat to phone. The police station nearby told us that a black woman, answering to my godmother's description, had collapsed and died in the street. They had taken her body to the morgue. The next day,

---

Pas-de-loup concerts, from the name of a French orchestra conductor

after a sleepless night, I went with the concierge and a friend to identify the body. It was Godmother. As she worked very near to where she lived, she never carried her identification papers on her, so as not to destroy them or risk losing them.

A month later, the concierge helped me to find a maid's room in the neighbourhood. I gave up our two roomed flat and some of the furniture to one of our relatives. I realised some time afterwards that I had been cheated on the re-sale value of the furniture. That did not bother me unduly because I had changed all my furniture. It would have been very difficult for me to continue to live in Godmother's little apartment, each object, each piece of furniture reminded me of her. One night I had woken thinking I heard her calling me. I thought I had seen the shape of a body in her bed next to mine ...

My life in the little maid's room was just like the one I had known with my godmother. I went to work, came straight home to lock myself in before dark. On Sundays I went to visit Godmother's same friends, so that the break would not be too sudden.

So until I met Mamadou I had lived very far indeed from any echo of the colonial world. Hence, independence or self-government were words which were quite new to me. Nevertheless I quickly grasped and analysed the facts. Six months later, I felt perfectly at ease. Of course I was for independence, which was more in keeping with my head-strong character. While Mamadou, who was afraid of losing some of his 'made in France' comforts, admitted he was a supporter of self-government. Outwardly he was pro-independence, but very lukewarm. Besides, he confessed to me that if he got a good position when he finished his studies, the political regime would matter little to him.

The most virulent defender of independence, one of Mamadou's fellow students, who had seen his father forced to do degrading tasks, humiliated and struck by whites, was left with a hatred for whites which made him tremble with rage whenever he spoke about them. This, however, did not prevent him from tenderly clasping the waist of his white girlfriend. A very pretty blonde, her name was Martine. She had broken with her family, who did not want to associate with blacks, and lived, ecstatically happy, with her 'man'. Perhaps, in that way she hoped to obtain for her fellow countrymen, by her love, a pardon for their crimes.

For a year Mamadou and I saw each other every weekend and during the vacation as well as on holidays. Mamadou was not very forthcoming about our future or his feelings toward me. I know he was proud to go out with me. All his friends had adopted me and openly complimented him on my good looks and my engaging manner. For my part, I loved him with all the ardour and intensity of a first and only love. In my eyes he was perfect. I had no relatives, few friends, so Mamadou became my whole world. During the week I did my work mechanically, waiting for Saturday with feverish impatience. One evening, to my surprise, Mamadou came to meet me as I left work, to tell me about his success. He had just obtained his law degree.

'I've got it! A few more months and I'll be going home ...'

'And what about me?' I asked, not concealing my distress very well.

'You too, naturally ... You know you are very important to me. I'm always afraid to seem like a *toubab*, by talking about things like that. If it will reassure you, I have never told another woman that I loved her.'

I was overwhelmed with happiness. I opened my mouth, but no sound came out. I was living a wonderful dream, Mamadou loved me, he was taking me to live in his country, in Africa.

After that, everything happened very quickly. We were married the first Saturday in September that year, only a few days before we took the boat for Africa. We took as much as we could with us, a whole set of household linen that my godmother had spent years collecting in preparation for my

13

marriage. The most impressive part of our luggage was made up of all the gifts for relatives: brothers, sisters, uncles, aunts, cousins – the number appeared at once astonishing and magnificent to me, an only child, an orphan, besides. We had been at sea for two days. I was happy, very happy.

After dinner, we went to see a girl, one of Mamadou's countrywomen, who was returning home too, after completing her studies. As she did not travel well at sea, she had been in bed since our departure from Europe. I had met her in Paris but she didn't belong to Mamadou's circle of friends, although she was from the same village. We had only ever exchanged greetings; she seemed antagonistic towards me. So I was not surprised at her behaviour during our visit. She spoke in their language the whole time, ignoring me, then, when we said goodbye, she said, this time in French, to Mamadou: 'I hope you have bought gorgeous presents for Awa. If I were her, I would not have forgiven you.'

Mamadou did not answer, he was visibly embarrassed and preoccupied, which heightened my curiosity. Who was this Awa? I did not stop pestering him with questions. For the sake of peace and quiet, he finally confessed that before leaving home to study in France, he had been married, as was the custom in his country, to a cousin, the eldest daughter of one of his mother's brothers and that he had a five-year-old daughter. The marriage was not really his doing, it had been arranged by the family.

I was expecting anything, but not that. That Mamadou had had another woman before me, that was possible; but that he was already a husband and father, that I could not comprehend. Would I have been more shocked if he had confessed to being a thief, a criminal? I don't know.

His admission devastated me, filled me with despair. I felt as if the world no longer existed, as if all life around me had suddenly stopped. I said nothing. My throat was tight, I was paralysed by what I had just heard. Mamadou continued speaking, he spoke for a long time, I could not tell you what

14

he said. I only heard a vague murmur. Was it his voice or the gushing of my blood as my heart beat violently? I thought I had found in Mamadou the family I missed, so I did not love him only as a lover, a husband. I transferred to him all the filial affection which was overflowing in me as well. Once, again, I felt the anguish of being an orphan. Lost, alone, in the world. I was totally confused.

When my father died, my grandmother explained to me that Papa had gone to heaven, because God needed him, a good and just man. I accepted the idea, knowing nothing about death. My distress soon disappeared. When my godmother died, because of my youth, I was full of hope in the future, my life was a serene dawn. I had been working for only a few days, I was waiting for 'Prince Charming', so I patiently put up with my loneliness. But this time, the future I had dreamed about was being slowly transformed into a painful present. I had placed all my trust, all my love in this man, who was such a deplorable coward.

It was not so much the fact that he had another wife that I resented, but that he had kept it from me.

When I came to my senses, my mind was made up: as soon as I got to his country, I would leave Mamadou to his family and return to France. The rest of the journey was painful. This homecoming to Africa, the land of my forefathers, I had imagined it in a hundred different ways, and it had become a nightmare. I no longer wondered how Mamadou's family would receive me: I knew I would be an intruder, out of place, lost. The other woman was with her daughter, surrounded by family who had chosen her and who protected her. And I, I was there, absurdly alone to face them, I was the stranger ...

10.00 a.m.

Hunger forces me to abandon my memories for a while. I cross the yard. Awa, on a piece of matting under the

15

mango-tree, is picking the rice. Diary is with her. The two other children are fighting over a mango with green flies on it. Ndeye is nowhere to be seen. Is she still lolling in bed, or has she gone to hang about God knows where? From snatches of conversation, overheard beneath my window, it seems she spent a good deal of her time going to see men she knew, who worked in government offices, to ask them for money. It is obvious that Mamadou's entire salary would not be adequate to support her following of *griots*, to pay for the quack *marabouts*, the jewels and the *boubous*. What does she give in return?

The kitchen is crowded with utensils, some are even on the ground as there are not enough shelves. I help myself to a big cup of very hot *kinkelibah*. There is no more bread. No bread. Was there any this morning? A ray of sunlight from the window casts a wide band of light on one of the walls. It lights up a mixture of grime, smoke, finger marks, mosquitoes killed or caught in the filth. There are too many cobwebs to count on the ceiling. The cement covering the earth has long since lost its original hue. The sink is chipped; the tap, whose cock had been replaced by a nail, is closed by a skilful contraption of string, which doesn't prevent it from leaking. The price of just one of Ndeye's *boubous* would have been enough to transform this kitchen into a very pleasant place. An intriguing cockroach crawls around my right foot which remains motionless. Why should I kill it, when that would do nothing to diminish the number of its fellows? It grows more bold, climbs onto my foot, then off again and runs away. I want to scratch the sole of my foot, but I don't. Calmly, I sip the scalding liquid which goes down into my empty stomach and makes me feel good.

I sense someone behind me, I turn around: it is Diary. She says nothing and goes away again. I know that Awa has sent her to see what I was doing. Am I not mad in their eyes? It is natural. I am being watched. Annoyed, I lose all the feeling of serenity I had had in the morning, drop the cup and its

16

contents and go back to my room. I want to scream. Why this sudden anger? I tear a bigger hole in my sheet at a spot where it was not properly mended. I like the noise the fabric makes as it rips. So I carefully tear the sheet into tiny pieces. That keeps me busy, entertains me and calms my anger. At noon, the smell of rice and fish, which I have had to get used to, makes me feel hungry again. I come out of my room. Around the family 'bowl' silence descends. I sit down, eat and go back to my room, lie down and fall asleep, calmed.

4.00 p.m.

I wake up sweating. The day is at its hottest. I go to the window to re-establish contact with the household. Awa is plaiting Diary's hair. She is stretched out between her legs. I yawn, bored. I don't feel like writing for the moment. I take my strips of sheet and tear them diligently into tiny squares. How long did I spend doing that, my mind a complete blank? The volume of cloth torn up like that is impressive. I made a bundle by tying the four corners of the second sheet together, go out and scatter all of it over the yard.

I am expecting cries, comments and I sit at my window to enjoy the scene. Awa opens her mouth, holding her jaw with one hand, the other on her hip. Her eyes meet mine. She says nothing, her silence is eloquent, she is no doubt thinking that I am getting worse. I burst out laughing and close my window. This evening, I am assailed by the saddest memories. My thoughts are frightful and confused. My night is a long nightmare, in which dream outlasts sleep and turns into obsession. Meanwhile, all around me, there is joy; it is the night of the *Maouloud*. Mamadou has gone to one of the holy cities to visit the *Marabout* with some friends. Ndeye of course, has gone with him ...

Helene lit a cigarette, inhaled deeply and savoured the smoke which she blew out through her mouth skillfully pursing her lips, as she breathed it in again through her nostrils. It was a very harmful way to smoke she knew. She allowed herself to drift, to get lost in a rare reverie. She never took the time to dream or even to just think about the past. She ordered her life 'watch in hand'. She was very immersed in the present and deliberately focused on the future. This evening, reading these lines, fragments of her own life came back to her and forced her to make comparisons.

Unlike the author of this diary, she had not had a lonely childhood. Her childhood had been happy, her parents were still living. Being the last of a family of twelve children, too frail and sickly to work in the fields, her parents had sent her at six to the best school in the town, eight kilometres from their village, a school run by nuns. They took children who were legitimate, baptised and whose parents had a good reputation. In the classroom, the white children were in the front rows, then came the mulattos and finally, the last bench, at the very back of the class, was reserved for blacks. Helene's place was in the darkest corner, at the end, against the wall; three other little black girls shared the same bench. Their parents were important socially, so the nuns paid attention to them. Helene, a peasant's daughter, in her ill-fitting clothes, was left to herself in her corner. But that did not prevent her from learning as fast as the others, to read, write and count, to sing childish songs which delighted her father because they were quite different from the secular tunes of the local village schools. At the time Helene did not understand a word of these songs and today she was aware of just how feeble they were. One of them came back to her:

> When baby Jesus went to school
> He carried his cross across his shoulders,
> When he knew his lessons
> They would give him sweets.

Helene saw herself once more during the last cane harvest before she left for France for the first time. The villagers all gathered on one property to cut the cane. Helene's job was to bring drink for the men. She held a bottle of rum and a glass. Her sister Rosette, stronger than she was, carried an earthenware jar filled with water. They went from one cane cutter to another. Helene offered each man a glass of rum which was swallowed in a single draught, then Rosette would give him a little water in half a calabash. The man rinsed his mouth and spat out the water. You could see the joy on each face, despite the sun; sweat ran down the men's glistening muscles. Nobody seemed to feel fatigue or the sharp edges of the cane leaves. Ti Louis, lucky fellow, the only one in the shade, made his drum talk, and from time to time he would shout a tune which was picked up by the others in unison. The women tied up the cane in bundles of about six pieces, then piled them up in heaps which were loaded onto ox carts. The carts left the village very early each morning, at three or four o'clock, so as to be among the first when the factory opened to sell the cane. The difficult time was bath-time in the evening. All the slices from the cane leaves felt like so many bites on which rum was being poured.

That was the same year that Helene spent a wonderful day at the seaside. The whole family had set out with the birds in single file behind Aunt Sonia and her huge pot of matoutou crabe balanced on her head. Mother brought up the rear with a demijohn of water. Her brothers carrying sling-shots, pretended to be big-game hunters, asking everyone to lower their voices so as not to startle the game. Rosette carried the basket with the fruits, the bottle of rum and other little things. Helene remembered too the sweet smell of magnolia blossoms mingled with the bewitching scent of the frangipanis. She would amuse herself by making flower necklaces as she trotted along behind Rosette. After a good hour's walk they reached the beach. Helene was always impressed by this immense expanse of water. The day went by without anyone worrying about time passing. In the evening, on the way back, they walked more slowly, talked less. But the same contented joy shone in their eyes …

There was a knock at the door. She checked to see who the visitor was through the peephole and opened it.

'Good evening, Helene. I saw your light, I was just passing …

'Hello Jacques. You are just in time to help.'

'Are you really moving?'

'As you see, I'm getting ready. Ousmane is coming back tomorrow and we are getting married in ten days. I've found a three-roomed apartment in a little patch of green, outside the town. You'll come and see us often, won't you?'

19

'I will ... Forgive me, but I must tell you that I don't approve of your marriage to Ousmane. You have always been a terrific girl, as an old friend, I am duty bound to tell you what I think. Then you can do what you want. Ousmane is very young, he is a good ten years younger than you are. To be sure, you don't look your age, you are more attractive than a younger girl. He is dazzled by your physical, material and intellectual ease and confidence. But for how long? In four or five years, when your menopause begins with all its discomfort, when his ardour for you has cooled, he won't abandon you but he will use your money to marry and take care of a second, young, wife. You will only have two choices: to leave him, hurt and rejected, or to agree to share him. What then?'

'You are funny when you play the part of the moralising big brother. I think there is a third possibility, we may get along perfectly.'

'And what about his family? You are a social worker, you know how clever mothers, sisters and aunts are at bringing a new wife into a son's life. The prospect of your house being invaded by an army of nephews, nieces and cousins doesn't put you off?'

'My dear Jacques, you are very sweet. I am going to put you out all the same; thank you for your kind words. If ever one day I should have the problems you've just described, I won't fail to come and cry on your shoulder. You are divorced, let me have my own experience as far as marriage is concerned ... Bye!'

Jacques went away, relieved at having performed a sacred duty. He was very fond of Helene and wanted to keep her from being disillusioned. He believed Ousmane's feelings for her were sincere. He also knew from experience that with time and outside pressures Ousmane would not remain faithful to his commitment. In spite of Helene's optimistic nature, he felt very afraid for her.

Helene closed the door after him somewhat nervously. She had gone over all the difficulties she could encounter. And the most important thing for her was the fact that, at forty, her desire to have a child could prove to be impossible. Ousmane cherished the same wish. Well, they would see. She banished these thoughts with a shrug and went back to her reading.

Thursday, August 24, 1961, 1.00 p.m.

Despite a very restless night, I feel fine today. I stayed in bed till lunch time. Ndeye and Mamadou have not come back yet. The radio is broadcasting the speech made by the head of government, from the holy city. I catch words: national effort, development, first four year plan, etc. Why does Awa turn the radio up so loud? Especially to listen to a speech she cannot understand a word of, since her French never got beyond her first few scarcely intelligibile efforts ... I go and search the living-room, hoping to find something to read. Apart from Ndeye's rosewater literature, there is the national daily from the previous day. I flick through the adventures of Kouan Ndoye 'The treasure of the Mossi', by Buster Diouf. Nothing of any substance. I go back to my room and pick up the notebook which is on my bed. I open it and allow the past to surge up in a flood of memories ...

The day I arrived in the country, nothing happened the way I had imagined it would. I was not coldly received by the family, quite the opposite. As soon as we had disembarked, a whole crowd of aunts, cousins, sisters, and even my rival, took me by the hand and kissed me. The women were all talking at once. The national language mingled with French. One of the aunts tapped me on the cheek, showering me with what were certainly words of welcome. I didn't understand a single word and contented myself with smiling. I lost Mamadou in the crowd. We were reunited half an hour later. After a twenty minute ride in an old black taxi with hard seats, we reached Thirty-third Street, Uncle Alassane's house, where we were to live. The women took charge of me.

For a moment I managed to forget my troubles. All around me there were nothing but smiling faces. I forced myself to smile with everyone too. Refreshments were served. I greeted any number of children of neighbours, of relatives, more or less distant, who had come to welcome us.

The local Imam took both my hands, palms upraised, recited a few verses of the Koran and, to my great astonishment, spat in my hands, which I passed over my face, as the other women did. About two hours after our arrival, the meal was served: a delicious dish of rice and fish, with *diwunor* a sort of melted butter. The one that I had eaten in Paris, at friends, resembled it only very distantly. Seated around the bowl I could dissect my rival at leisure. She put the best pieces before me, smiling at me so insistently that I wondered if it were from kindness or from mockery. In any case I decided on a truce, especially since, having refused the spoon I was offered, I had to concentrate on making little balls of rice which I then put into my mouth, like the others. Although my desire to leave was very strong I had to yield to the reality that it was not going to be a simple matter. In fact, the expenses of our journey had swallowed up almost all our savings. We had just enough money to live very frugally until Mamadou found a job.

After we had eaten, I was able to see Mamadou alone, in the little room which we had been given. Once more I tried very calmly to bring up the subject of our separation, because for me that was the only real solution. I did not want half a husband, neither did I want to take a little girl's father away from her. Mamadou refused to see my point of view.

'You are making a mountain out of something insignificant ... I was forced to marry Awa because the family had arranged it from when I was very young. The only woman that I chose, that I love, is you ... My one concern is to find a job and a place to live as quickly as possible. Everything else is secondary.'

When this long tirade was over, far from being reassured, I wondered what love meant for Mamadou. I could not understand that he could have married someone simply to please his family ... I did not want to believe that he had the dishonesty not to tell me before our marriage and, now, the audacity to be surprised that I should refuse to accept a situation that I had not chosen.

After eight days of this ambiguity, Uncle Alassane, with whom we were living, had a talk with Mamadou and communicated to him the decisions and wishes of the family: they would accept my coming most willingly, but on no account would they agree to a separation from Awa who had waited for him faithfully for five years. Awa had gone back home to her native village, to Mamadou's parents' house, where she had been living since her marriage. From the next weekend on Mamadou would have to go to her. Mamadou told me that he had no choice, and that if we refused we would be ostracised by the whole community, that it would be impossible for us to live in the country and that he had absolutely no intention of going to live anywhere else. So, he proposed that I should agree until he got a job and a place for us to live; then he would find a reason to break with Awa. In short, I was to accept having a husband for five days, since Awa agreed to have him on weekends in the village. It seemed to me that I was on another planet, for I no longer understood what was going on around me, what was being said. As far as I was concerned, a husband was above all the most intimate of beings, another self, not an object to be lent or shared.

In a week Mamadou became a different person, a stranger I had just met. I no longer understood his reactions. I was choking with anguish and with unprecedented rage. He remained very calm, happy to be alive, to have come back home to his country and his friends. He would carry on conversations for hours in his native language, with no regard for me. We had to pay a great number of visits to friends and relatives. Whenever we went out he would introduce me, then forget me in a corner, like some discarded object, surrounded by a group of women who were smiling and kind, but who spoke no French. I saw him at a distance, chatting with the men. Neither could I understand this sort of segregation where women seemed to have no importance in a man's life, except for his pleasure or as the mother of children. They were not companions and confidantes. An aura of mystery surrounded the affairs of the husband who, as sole master, made all the decisions without ever worrying about the wishes and desires of the women. The wives, ignorant of their husbands' real financial means, spent their time vying with each other as to the number of outfits and jewels they had, the messenger's wife wanting to have as many as the director's. This sometimes created tragic situations when at the end of a month a husband found himself with debts which far exceeded his total salary.

Constantly tense, on edge, I had no appetite. The delicious midday rice and fish, with daily repetition, no longer tasted as it had the first day. The smell of it nauseated me. I was losing weight, my skirts, which now were too big, made me look like a scarecrow. So when it was time for Mamadou's first weekend with Awa I was in a sorry state, physically and mentally. I tried to accept it, telling myself that in any case it was all over between us; that as soon as I had the chance I would go back to France. I would get a divorce. However it was too much for me to bear. I remained locked in our room without eating or drinking. Mamadou did not come back on Sunday evening as expected, he arrived on Monday at lunchtime, looking happy.

'Awa sends her regards, the family too,' he said, smiling.

'You can do without giving me a message like that,' I replied.

In spite of all my resolutions I was dying of jealousy. I could not keep myself from thinking of Mamadou with another woman as a sacrilege. Mamadou my only treasure, my most precious possession! When I married him, it was more than a husband, it was a whole family that I had found. He had become the father who had died too soon, the friend whom I had always dreamed of. I had never kept anything about myself from him; even my present pain and sorrow, I

24

did not have the decency to hide from him.

The second weekend, my anguish was so acute that I lost all notion of time. Today, I can remember nothing, it is as if I was unconscious for two days.

The third weekend when Mamadou left for Awa's, his uncle took me to the hospital. I was deeply depressed, really raving or to use the doctor's expression I suffered 'fits of delirium'. I do not know what happened to me. I vaguely remember being overcome with a sudden, desperate rage during the night between Sunday evening and Monday morning. I began breaking everything in my room and banging my head against the walls. I did not come to my senses completely until four days later in the hospital. Aunt Khady, uncle Alassane's wife was standing next to my bed. She explained to me as best she could, with lots of gesticulating, what I was doing there. It was a Thursday. I had been in a semi-conscious state for four days, probably because of the injections I had been given to calm me. I felt good, my mad rage had given me relief, the rest-cure had done me good. Mamadou arrived. His presence irritated me. I could not understand how the man I had loved, that I still loved, had in so short a time become this stranger. For a year we had been together and he had never mentioned his first family nor this child who was his daughter. Why? What I blamed him for most of all was that he had hidden the truth from me. He had not shouldered his responsibilities and then he had waited for the family and uncle Alassane to make all the decisions. What a pathetic case! Or was I the one who was being unreasonable? I was surprised at the behaviour of the people around me. The very ground seemed to be crumbling under my feet, I was struggling in a strange, irrational world.

I wonder if it was a good thing to have started this diary, to be trying to remember a past more filled with sorrows than with joys; to dwell on a present built on troubles, on solitude, despair and on a vague feeling of acceptance of a numb existence to which the regrets and resentments of the past have given way? Stirring up all that, isn't it provoking a sleeping tiger?

Ndeye's laughter and raucous, unpleasant voice bring me back to everyday reality. She is back from their visit to the Marabout; Mamadou and two colleagues who travelled with them are back as well. They are in the drawing room. I hear the clinking of glasses which Ndeye is taking from the sideboard. In spite of the household's financial difficulties there is always enough to buy beer, Ndeye's favourite drink, and Mamadou's whisky. Mamadou's two colleagues won't leave until the bottle of Scotch is empty. Ndeye, for once very astute, divides a new bottle in two or three and never gives those two a full bottle, since she knows their practices very well. Yet they have just celebrated *Maouloud* meditating and reciting the holy Koran. Apparently they are good Moslems; at home, they keep no alcohol, so as not to shock their families, besides it is more economical to drink at someone else's house. Mamadou, who is more candid in this matter, buys his whisky and drinks it openly in his own house. At his parents' I suspect he is just as hypocritical. Yes, everything is a show, the essential is to appear rich, generous, temperate, a good Moslem, open and honest, a good husband. Meanwhile you are stone broke, selfish, alcoholic, lying, you never take care of your children and you neglect your wives. Only the latest wife counts, the empty-headed creature whom you call a modern woman, whom you shower with jewels. I hear snatches of their conversation. Mamadou says he is thinking of going to France for his next leave with Ndeye who is dying to see Paris. I can't hear what the others say. All the same I wonder where he thinks he will get the money for this trip. As for me, I never dream of Paris or anywhere else any more. I have buried once and for all everything that goes on outside this house. My life unfolds in a room five paces by four and under the mango tree in the

yard where I eat my meals. Once more the radio is blaring –
this time the eight o'clock news. I exchange my newspaper
for my bed. No shower, no dinner either, as long as the
visitors are in the house – I don't remember if Mamadou
asked me to do that, I think I decided on it on my own –
except when it comes to Ndeye's friends who always sit under
my window in the courtyard and who disturb me with their
gossip. Then I do my best to scandalise them.

*The more Helene read the more she felt drawn towards this woman. She
felt her suffering and the difference between them. She was sure she
could never love a man to the point where she lost her reason over him.
Her love affair in Paris, when she was twenty, had proved to be a real
vaccination, which protected her perfectly against falling in love.*

*At the time she had believed a fellow countryman's declarations of
love. He had formally asked for her hand in marriage. They had even
exchanged letters with their respective families. Their parents had
arranged a big dinner party back home in honour of their engagement.
Helene was in her second year at the school of social work in Paris and
Hector in his third year of medical school. They had agreed to wait two
years before marrying, long enough to allow Helene to finish her studies
and to work for a year in order to save something towards setting up
house. The two years went by quickly and uneventfully.*

*Two months before the wedding day Hector had sent his best friend
to announce to Helene that he had been married the previous day to a
French girl who was expecting his child. He had not wanted to tell her
because he wanted to save them both from a painful scene. To top it all
off, he had the nerve to say that the marriage was a matter of honour
and that he still loved her.*

*Helene had forced herself to keep her dignity, to hold her head high
and not to cry in front of his friend. She looked at him with contempt.
'The hypocritical little black, full of complexes, who thinks by
marrying a white woman he is acquiring a passport to success!' she
thought to herself. 'And isn't it a matter of honour when you have been
engaged to a childhood sweetheart for two years?'*

When Hector's friend departed, Helene had locked herself into her room for two days with her grief; weeping, moaning, cursing Hector, giving full vent to her disappointment. When she managed to compose herself, her mind was made up. A woman could live by herself. She had sworn never again to suffer because of a man. She made a bonfire in her bathroom sink with Hector's letters and photos and barricaded her heart with a block of ice. She asked to be transferred overseas. Since then she had worked in several African countries. She had set out to pay Hector back through every man she met. She would use them for a while, then as soon as they seemed to be becoming involved, she would stop seeing them without any explanation. She had agreed to marry Ousmane because she wanted a child and because in accordance with her old-fashioned ideas, she preferred the child to be born in a legitimate union. One thing for sure, she thought, she would never put up with any infidelity on Ousmane's part.

Helene lit another cigarette. She had started smoking to look emancipated and liberated and had acquired a taste for it. Now she smoked two packets a day. She intended to stop one of these days, it was the only concession she would make to Ousmane, who did not smoke. She went to the kitchen to pour herself a whisky on the rocks. Her parents had been scandalised, the last time she was home on holiday, because she preferred to have whisky rather than their delicately-flavoured little punches.

She had seen Hector again for the first time since their broken engagement. He had settled in their homeland and had a successful medical practice. She had accepted an invitation to dinner at his house out of curiosity, to see the kind of woman he had preferred to her. He had introduced here as a childhood friend, without mentioning their previous relationship.

Hector's wife was a small blonde, dumpy, faded, dressed like a scarecrow, without charm; she seemed much older than her years. She did not work but looked after her home and her six children. She fussed constantly after her offspring who were particularly turbulent and indisciplined.

He told Helene, as he took her back home, how much he regretted not having married her. His life, it appeared, was a living hell. Helene had burst out laughing. No, there was no way Hector could move her, she

28

had her block of ice firmly in place around her heart. She had told him about her life in Africa, free, pleasant and with no ties. Then to amuse herself, she had excited him. They made love in the car, on the beach. Skillfully she had managed to keep him with her until the small hours of the morning so as to infuriate his good wife, and then left him sheepish and drained. She had accepted an invitation to see him again a few days later, but had not gone. She had not seen him again during her stay on the island.

Smiling at the memory of the trick she had played on Hector, Helene went to lie down, fully dressed, her glass near at hand, and buried herself, once more in her young compatriot's diary.

Friday, August 25, 1961, 7.00 a.m.

Like every morning, the first thing I do is open my window, scan the sky through the branches of the mango tree and watch the household getting up. It is hot and the flies are already buzzing around. I am sweating. Last night I fell asleep before the visitors left, I did not get the chance to shower. So, this morning I hurry to the shower so I can get there first. The water is cool on my skin, like a gentle caress. It is a good feeling; I forget about myself, I am lulled into sleep, I dream about streams and waterfalls. I am back in my island, a child again, on the banks of a clear-running stream. I wade in, my weariness dissolves in the cool water. My heart swells with happiness. This is the first time since I have been here that I have thought about my homeland. Usually the memories that come back to me are of my life in France.

I am snatched from my reverie and brought abruptly back to the present by someone hammering on the door, uttering the usual pleasantries: the word 'mad' recurs like a leitmotiv. I open the door with the water still running. Mamadou is staring at me, suddenly silent, visibly startled and fascinated. My body is still beautiful and desirable ... I fill my mouth with water, spit it in his face and close the door. Today, he will have to be satisfied with washing his face the way a cat does, I have made up my mind to stay in the shower until he leaves the house. He will not dare to evict me forcibly.

I come out as soon as I hear his car driving off. As I walk across the yard, Awa looks at me. I stop and look her in the eye. She lowers her eyes and mumbles, no doubt something about my madness getting worse. Back in my room, I throw myself across my bed. Mamadou's eyes have reawakened in my memory moments of tenderness which I thought I had forgotten forever. Goodbye to peace and quiet, once again here I am, filled with passionate longing. I am warm, despite the shower, I am perspiring. My heart beats faster and faster. I am in agony, my whole body trembles, I shatter into thousands of tiny pieces. My spirit is deeply troubled and I am painfully aware of my loneliness. I want to die ... No, I must not die. Ndeye would be too happy to see me dead and she is the last person I want to please. As for Mamadou, my death would relieve him of the burden. I am on his conscience ...

9.30 a.m.
After an hour spent day-dreaming, I come back to the concrete reality of my diary. Friend and confidante. Thanks to my diary, I discover that my life is not in pieces, that it had only been coiled deep down inside of me and now comes back in huge raging waves, to jog my memory. For years I had wavered between abject depression and raging despair with no one to turn to. It had never occurred to me that putting down my anguish on a blank page could help me to analyse it, to control it and finally, perhaps to bear it or reject it once and for all.

The day after I woke up in the hospital, after the doctor had been to see me a nurse came for me. She took me from the hut where I had been alone to a room in the main building. There were two beds; in one, a young woman, who stared at

30

me apparently without seeing me. I said good morning as I came in. She did not answer, probably still lost in her own thoughts. I got into the empty bed. Several minutes later, coming back from her long distant journey, my companion said to me: 'You are not from here either, I can tell'.

'No, I come from the islands. And you?' I asked.

'I am a child of the water. Soon I will go back to the banks of my river, the Congo … Here, there is no water, look how dry everything is all around us. I am thirsty, nothing can quench my thirst.'

Then she began to laugh mockingly and to sob at the same time, softly, bitterly. There were no tears in her eyes; from time to time she spoke in what must have been her own language. She remained like that the whole day. In the evening she had a lot of visitors, probably school friends from the university in town where she was a philosophy student. As long as her friends were there, my companion seemed to feel better about life; she smiled and talked. After her friends left she offered me the tit-bits that they had brought her.

Mamadou came very late. I couldn't think of anything to say to him. Apart from 'Hello, how are you feeling?' he didn't say three words either. So we sat for the length of the visit each lost in our own throughts like an old couple spending a long evening together. I pictured myself knitting socks while Mamadou did crossword puzzles. The idea made me smile. I knew that this vision of a quiet, uneventful future could in no way resemble the life of a couple in this country. Here, a couple is never alone together, the family is there, surrounding you, distracting you, thinking of you, thinking for you.

Mamadou went off again, asking if I needed anything in particular that he could bring me the next day. No, I didn't need anything. I closed my eyes. I was floating on a cloud high up above earth. The injections probably had a lot to do with my state of tranquil indifference. I fell asleep lulled by my neighbour's deep snoring. In the middle of the night I thought I heard sobs and cries. But I was too drugged with

31

sleep to know whether it was a dream or not.

The next day I had an interview with the doctor. She was a young French woman, very pleasant with a reassuring smile. I felt at ease. She listened, questioned me about my life in this country, my plans for the future and offered to help me if I wanted to be repatriated to France (this was a possibility I had not known existed). Finally, she told me that all I needed was a little rest and prescribed tranquilizers to help me sleep. I spent a few more days in the hospital; mainly, I slept. I did not get out of bed except when I absolutely had to. The food was worse than Uncle Alassane's daily rice and fish. I had refused to have my meals brought for me from home and I swallowed everything without even bothering about the taste, adding more salt or sugar than I needed to.

The following Saturday I went back home to the uncle who lived in Thirty-third Street. Mamadou had just got a job in a bank, thanks to his uncle's good offices, and was to begin an orientation period on Monday. One of his friends had found us a garden apartment, in a busy street in the town-centre. The prospect of a place of our own made the next two weeks quite bearable. At last, one Sunday, we moved into our little two-roomed apartment. We had ordered furniture from a local cabinet-maker. We already had dishes, household linen and a gas stove brought back with us from France. We decided to buy something useful for the house every month until we had everything we needed. We had worked out a strict budget for all our expenses, including what we were to give to relatives in the village, and even in Thirty-third Street where I did not really think our help was needed, since Uncle Alassane had a good pension from the government and his children were working. But he had been the one who brought up Mamadou, who had sent him to school: we owed him a debt of gratitude. So we had to deprive ourselves, when necessary, of essentials so that Uncle could have extras.

Mamadou took over the responsibility for his younger

brothers' schooling and living expenses. He was relatively well paid. Still, we did not have anything left over for savings, which did not please me. After my discharge from the hospital he no longer talked of weekends in the village nor of wanting to divorce Awa or me. I must admit that he was making an effort to help me to forget the difficulties we had had. In the evenings, immediately after work, he would come and take me for long walks along the seashore. Or sometimes we would go to visit friends. He tried not to have conversations in his native language which I still did not understand, and patiently tutored me in the ways and customs of his tribe. I too tried to learn to talk with the aunts and girl cousins who did not understand French.

I thought, at this stage, that my troubles were over. I became my old self again, confident, trusting, kind, good-natured. Then three months later we had a very happy event. It was the day I went to see the doctor because I was not feeling well. He gave me the news that I would be a mother in six months, if all went well. I had never before had even the slightest false alarm. Knowing that I was to be a mother changed my whole way of looking at things. My main preoccupation was to prepare for the coming of the baby. Nothing else mattered for me any more. Mamadou had never been so attentive. He watched over my diet, urging me to eat more and more, under the pretext that I was eating for two. He confessed that one of the reasons why he had not wanted to divorce his first wife was the fear that I might not have been able to give him children. For him, having children was the greatest blessing in a marriage. During this period we were very happy in our life together, full of affection for each other. This lasted for two months. For me, the only cloud on our happiness continued to be the numerous visits from aunts, uncles, cousins, on all sides. They never left before meal time, in fact quite the opposite, they would often arrive just in time to sit down to eat. Since I did not feel like preparing rice and fancy African sauces

33

every day, I was obliged to perform clever feats to feed these visitors. Moreover, more often than not we had to give them money for the taxi home. Sometimes we were asked for a loan to solve a problem which was always urgent. This loan, of course, was never repaid ...

Still, everything was working out for the best in the best of all worlds on this radiant April morning. Carrying my basket, I was skipping along from stall to stall in the market. From one vendor to the next the vegetbles seemed fresher and better, the prices too were very different. Because of my timidity, I could not get used to the classic habit of bargaining in African markets. All the vendors were calling out to me at the same time. 'Pretty lady, come this way; come over here and see; I will give you a good price; my tomatoes are prettier, just like you.'

Leaving the market, I stopped for a minute to look at the sky. It was a beautiful deep, cloudless blue. As happy as could be, I started across the avenue by the market when suddenly something hit me on my left side. For a brief moment I was conscious of lying flat on the ground on top of my tomatoes and of feeling a severe dull pain which gripped my abdomen. Then I fainted.

When I came to, I found myself in a hospital bed. The woman next to me called the nurse.

'What happened to me?' I asked.

'Don't upset yourself, it's nothing,' the nurse told me.

'I don't feel good! Oh! It hurts so much.'

'Don't worry, you are going to be all right,' she assured me.

I was half-dazed. I knew I was speaking yet I didn't understand anything I was saying. Afterwards I heard that I had been knocked down by a car. The driver wasn't going fast but I was looking at the sky as I stepped out into the street. I was out of danger, to be sure, but I had had an operation and I had lost my baby. When Mamadou got there, I was overcome with weeping and despair. Mamadou did his best to console me, assuring me that it was nothing. 'We will have one, lots of others ...'

Two weeks after the accident I left the hospital. I was to rest at home for a few days and go back for a check-up. I cheered up. After all, I was only twenty-two and my life was ahead of me. One of Mamadou's nieces, Mariama, came to see me and told me that the accident was the work of the *Marabout* that Awa had been visiting in the village, since Mamadou had stopped going to see her. In addition, the baby clothes that I had been knitting in preparation for the birth had contributed to my misfortune.

Here, the custom was that one should not prepare for the coming of a child. The clothes were bought after the birth. So, oftentimes the baby spent the first hours of his life wrapped in the *pagne* that the mother was wearing at the delivery.

I refused to believe these superstitions, still, what she told me disturbed me a lot. Who knows ...? Our joy had indeed been extremely short-lived. Mamadou had become edgy, irritable; he started coming home late and spent all his evenings with his friends. As for me, I was living in a state of constant distress, trying at the same time to cling to false hopes. A month went by, painfully, an eternity of long empty, boring days. I went for my check-up. The doctor who examined me told me I was fine, but remained very evasive when I asked about another pregnancy. It was then that Mamadou admitted that the doctor had told him that there was no chance that I would ever have another child. He had not told me before because he had wanted to give me time to get well first.

This confession was like a death-knell to my hopes of happiness, to my zest for living. Mamadou, as I expected, resumed his weekend visits to Awa. He was going to the village simply to see his mother, he said. He even asked me to go with him. Nothing was of the slightest interest to me any more. Apart from Mamadou, I had no one. I clung to him desperately, aware that he could not shield me from the whirlwind which threatened to engulf my reason.

One day Mamadou announced that he was trying to find a bigger house so that he could bring Awa to live in town. Her daughter was to start school the next term and he would need to look after her. I was really alone, my whole body ached and no medicine could ease my pain. Violent migraines made me sick. I withdrew completely into my sorrow, spending days and days without going out, without eating, turning over and over the same thoughts, harking back to the same old story, endlessly, until I became numb, distraught. I no longer opened my door to visitors. Mamadou had his own key and sometimes he would find a relative waiting behind the door. I became voluble whenever I drank. I would drink in secret, hoping that way to assuage my grief, to stop thinking, but I did not like alcohol and soon I gave up the attempt. I used tears, tantrums, special dishes, coquetry, indifference, to try to dissuade Mamadou from bringing Awa to town. His mind was made up. Whenever we discussed it, he tried to persuade me to accept this very natural solution; if I would only show good will our life would be very pleasant as Awa was simple, sweet, self-effacing. Nothing between us would change, moreover, he wouldn't have to go away every weekend, we would be a big, happy family, Awa's children would be my children. Mamadou thought my unhappiness was just a matter of a stubborn whim. For my part, the situation was, and would remain, inconceivable. I had thoughts which made me shudder with horror. I suffered, I thought about suicide, I couldn't make up my mind to do it. Not for fear of the physical pain, but because this solution was against my moral and religious principles which held that life was sacred. I threw myself into prayer, meditation, novenas to all sorts of saints. I went from mass to mass. I didn't even know what I really wanted: live with Mamadou, leave him, leave his country? Everything inside me was in turmoil. The one thing that was real, this suffering which I could not understand, unbalanced my mind, gave everything I put to my lips the taste of earth and made my stomach turn over like a ploughed field.

The day of Awa's arrival, her sisters, cousins, friends, came with her from the village. They had rented a bus and even brought a drummer. Apparently indifferent, I suffered at this festivity, clenching my teeth to keep from screaming. Awa moved into our present house first, since Mamadou could not afford to pay two sets of rental. Then despite my reticence, a few days later I came to live like an intruder in Awa's home. She welcomed me with great kindness, I must admit. A woman who was naturally soft, generous and submissive, polygamy was a part of her culture; she willingly accepted sharing her husband. She seemed really happy to be living in town with her husband at last. Her happiness revolted me.

After a week of living together, I could no longer stand Mamadou. I had reached the depths of the absyss of my misfortune.

> *Fill my lamp with oil, oh Lord,*
> *Light up my long night from the depths of this pit.*

> *Fill my lamp with oil, oh Lord,*
> *Make my dark and sorrowful soul to shine.*

> *Fill my lamp with oil, oh Lord,*
> *This world is full of shadows, this pit so dark.*

> *Fill my lamp with oil, oh Lord,*
> *From my heart full of bitterness banish the darkness.*

I rambled, begged, bombarded the Eternal one with ardent prayers. I decided I would no longer share Mamadou's bed and I moved into my present room, which had originally been for the children. I cut off all my hair and put on mourning clothes. It was a way of finally crushing any hope that was still left within me. Mamadou thought that I had really lost my mind. I did nothing to dissuade him. For the first time, he offered to let me leave. It was too late. The whole world was like a barren, hostile desert and I was struggling in the depths of an abyss, alone, defenceless. My fingers were plunged in a thick mud which stuck to my clothing, my skin. I spent hours, even the entire day and sometimes the whole night, under the shower, soaping myself, but I could not get rid of it. Mamadou took me to a psychiatrist and I had an electro-encephalogram. The doctor, a man this time, apparently understood nothing of my problem. He talked mainly with Mamadou, prescribed medication, rest, quiet, and a nutritious diet. I had lost so much weight that my clothes were floating about me, like everything else around me. I no longer saw anyone else, the only thing that mattered was my pain. I moulded it and shaped it with the clay from the pit into which my sorrow had cast me. I no longer took part in any activity outside of my room, I no longer went out. I was becoming like a vegetable.

Awa was the real mistress of the house. I could find no fault with her. When she came home from the hosptial after the birth of her baby son Alioune, she came to see me and told me: 'Take him, he is yours'. I was touched that she should entrust me with her baby. Nevertheless I could feel her deep anxiety, for I could read in her eyes her fear as to what my reaction would be; yet to please me she could transcend her fear. She did everything to make me feel comfortable, genuinely surprised at my behaviour, not understanding my refusal to have my husband in my bed on the three days which were mine by right ...

The day of Alioune's baptism, she insisted that I should stay in the yard with her friends. Not one of them spoke French. The way they laughed at everything, the things they said to me which I didn't understand, became in my head so many jeers, taunts which echoed with such resonance that I could not keep myself from stopping up my ears. This apparently had no effect.

Mamadou strutted majestically, moving from one group to another. He was wearing a magnificent white *boubou*, richly embroidered, and immaculate white slippers. He was handsome. A handsome monster, selfish, proud on his day of glory. His virility confirmed, his line assured, he was baptising his first son. It was to experience this moment that he had sacrificed me. He shook hands warmly with the women seated next to me and spoke to them amicably. He took my hand, mechanically, without even gracing me with a look. Had I become a zombie? He no longer saw me. As the hours went by I felt myself melting away; like ice in the sun. About mid-day I felt as if I was as small as an ant.

I looked at the people who surrounded me; they were frightful giants, with monstrous faces. A woman got up, began to laugh, her mouth wide open. She had two gold teeth; to me they were two fangs shining in the mouth of a Sphinx. I felt afraid. I got up staggering, and with great difficulty made my way to my room. I could not leave my bed for the rest of the day. As soon as I tried to get up, my head began to spin in a whirl. Awa, visibly distressed, came once or twice to see how I was feeling.

As for Mamadou, he did not budge. I knew exactly why I was hurting at that moment. Mamdou's happiness made me sad. If I had had the child he wanted so much, our life would have been quite different. I felt like crying. I was weeping inside, without shedding a tear, I was weeping for my loneliness in the midst of all this celebration. I was weeping over Mamadou, so happy, who, in this moment of joy, was not thinking of the pain that he was causing me and which he would pay for one day. To get revenge, I imagined him dead, nothing but a fine stinking corpse, on which I spat. This image made me burst out laughing, a ridiculous, demented, laugh which left me breathless. Then my tears flowed and I fell asleep calmed.

39

After that, I never took part in any of the household festivities. I would lock myself in my room as soon as visitors appeared. Oulimata's baptism, two years later, was celebrated without fuss. She was a girl ...

3.00 p.m.

I love Awa's children, they are they children I would like to have had. At the beginning, visibly afraid that I would harm them, she avoided leaving them alone with me. In time, she understood that my resentment did not extend to the children, that I loved them. This feeling, which was reciprocated by the children, certainly influenced the way Awa behaved towards me. She looked after me like a mother, sometimes she had a dress made for me by her tailor. She bought me whatever little things I might need. She was the only person in the house apart from the children to whom I spoke ...

The children often come to see me in my room. Diary, the eldest, is already very pretty; she is about ten. During the school year, she sometimes asks me to hear her lessons; she shows me her exercise books when she gets a good mark. Alioune is almost exactly the age that the child I lost would have been, so he is my favourite. He does not go to school yet, but he has learnt French from me; I have always spoken to him in French since he was very young. The youngest, Oulimata, is just two and will certainly be as pretty as her sister.

About two years ago, Mamadou had married a third wife, who is really the second, for I have retired from the 'competition' and only take part very distantly in the life of the household. Ndeye, the new wife, hates me and is always directing insults in my direction. Why? I never look at her, I never hear her either. I ignore her, and that is perhaps what annoys her so much, having to talk to herself. She is the one who christened me 'the mad woman'.

Mamadou is at home less and less. From time to time he comes to see how I am. I always receive him in the same way since he brought Ndeye here. He talks to himself, I never answer any of his questions ...

After Independence, a fellow country woman, a social worker, who heard about my difficulties in adapting to life in the country came to see me to offer to have me repatriated to France. She came back again, but I refused to see her, rightly or wrongly. I can't see what I would go back to Paris to do. I have no desires, no family, no really close friends. I have become accustomed to my vegetable life. I wonder, if I had to leave this house, how I would go about resuming normal life and healthy relationships with other people. Ndeye's malice and hatred and Mamadou's cowardice are a part of the normal cycle of my life and that makes no difference to me. I married Mamadou for better or for worse. In spite of my initial reaction which was to leave him, he is all the family I have, so I accept this worse. I am no longer the woman in his life. Was I ever? Is there a woman who really matters to him? Awa is the mother of his children, Ndeye his partner in debauchery. How does he feel about me now? He puts up with me, I am the family scourge, the leper whom they hide and feed for love of Allah, the stranger who Mamadou made the mistake of bringing home. The family, never having adopted me, did not need to reject me. Aunt Khady alone comes to greet me when she comes to the house. The others ignore me.

They have apparently accepted Ndeye without reservation. She is a daughter of their country, so, worthy of their son. Yet, according to Awa, Ndeye, a flighty girl, had already had a husband and countless love affairs. Mamadou was just one among the many lovers. He married her purely out of vanity because she was much sought after. It seems Mamadou borrowed a considerable sum of money to meet the expenses occasioned by his marriage to Ndeye. The bedroom was redecorated in accordance with the taste and liking of the new wife: it was the same room I had shared with Mamadou earlier in our marriage.

The day Ndeye arrived, I had carefully locked myself in my room. I watched part of the festivities from behind my shutters. There was no comparison to Awa's arrival, which it turned out had been extremely modest. Ndeye and her friends were like walking jewellery stores, their *boubous* were sumptuous. Bank notes changed hands at a stunning rate, the *griots* vied with each other in their inventiveness. Singing and dancing went on for a very long time. For at least three days the house was never empty of noisy visitors.

About a week later, our first encounter as co-wives, or at least as co-occupants of the same house, took place, witnessed by Awa. I was coming out of the shower, Ndeye offered me her hand, I did not take it. I greeted Awa and went my way. I had decided to ignore this woman totally, and Mamadou as well. Then she said to Awa:

'She really is mad ... Why does Mamadou keep her here?'

'She doesn't bother anybody,' Awa replied.

'All the same, I can't stand people who are crazy. She is going to have to stay out of my way, because I can't bear strange people.'

'If you don't look at her, she won't look at you either,' said Awa, walking away to put an end to the discussion.

Mamadou came up and spoke very softly to Ndeye, who answered: 'I have just met your *toubabesse*. She is crazier than I imagined her, she refused to say good morning.'

I was fuming, furious about this girl, whose very appearance I did not like. She was the type that they call here a 'beautiful woman' because she was tall, well-covered with flesh. I preferred Awa's type: medium height, fine features, noble bearing. And here I was, as far as she was concerned, crazy, and what was just as annoying to me, 'European' or *toubabesse*. She was quite simply identifying me with the white wives of the colonials. She was even stripping me of my identity as a black woman. My

42

forefathers had paid dearly for my right to be black, spilling their blood and giving their sweat in hopeless revolts to enrich the soil of the Americas so that I might be born free and proud to be black.

In France, I had never been offended when people referred to my colour. I remember I always accepted proudly the fact that I was different, all the more so as very often I had heard people say as I passed: 'She is a pretty black woman' or 'The little black girl is adorable'. Then, I would never have imagined that on African soil I would have been called a white woman. This insult wounded me deeply and increased my antagonism towards Ndeye. I knew that from that day on I would feel nothing but contempt and resentment towards her.

Mamadou, as always, said nothing and moved away. I was at the window in my room. For the first time Ndeye looked at me cruelly and followed Mamadou towards the living room.

Helene regretted that she had not been more insistent about looking after this young compatriot who had been in trouble. It was Doctor Monravi, a French psychiatrist, who had spoken to her about her, knowing she was from the islands. On her second visit, Mamadou's young wife had refused to see her and had locked herself in her room. Really overworked, she had not gone back there and had forgotten about her. About four years later a colleague, the social worker at the psychiatric hospital, had spoken to her again about this woman who was back in hospital for quite a long stay. Her colleague had asked her to try to find someone from the young woman's family when she went home to the islands on vacation. Helene had indeed met a great-aunt and some cousins, but they had had no news of Mamadou's wife since she had left the island as a child. Of course they did not envisage taking on the responsibility of an unknown relative, one who was ill besides. Helene found it difficult to judge them; she was asking them to take on a big responsibility.

Helene poured herself another scotch, lit another cigarette. It was already two o'clock. She was not sleepy and she was not working the following day; so she could spend the night in any way she wanted. Something else which it would be hard for her to do after her marriage. She wondered, deep down, why she had decided to get married after so many years. She did not find it difficult to be alone; when she was very young she had always been surrounded by her many brothers and her sister Rosette. Since she had left her island to further her studies, she had lived alone and saw only the advantages in her present life-style. Her friends thought her good company. She had taken on a self-protective shell of cynicism, deliberately numbing herself in order not to take to heart the suffering of others which she had to try to assuage every day. This young compatriot's story reminded her of a case she had followed the year before: A woman recently married. The husband emigrates to France to work, she is to join him as soon as possible. When she arrives, a few months later, she finds one of her friends and neighbours, who had left the country at the same time as her husband, in the house, living with her husband. Alone, far from her family, from her home, she cannot stand the shock. She becomes ill. The husband sends her home to her parents who live in the area where Helene works. The goitre which her distress had provoked responds to no treatment. She dies of no other apparent cause except a broken heart.

Normally, Helene avoided thinking about it, so as not to arrive at the following conclusion: all men, regardless of their level of culture or their social origin, were complete egotists who were not worth shedding a single tear over. She was aware that by marrying her Ousmane was making a good match, all sentiment aside. She earned four or five times more than he did, because of her expatriate contract, had a little apartment in Paris, a summer house in the islands built next to her family home, which her sister Rosette, who had been widowed prematurely, occupied with her four children. Of Helene's ten brothers, the two eldest had been killed in France in the Second World War. There was no sign of three others who had left to work abroad. Five had stayed on the land and were cane-farmers on the family property. They had married girls from the village and had raised large families of children whom Helene could not tell apart. Whenever she went on holiday, she took a suitcase full of toys and clothes of all different sizes.

44

In their eyes she was the pretty career-woman, the aunt that they all waited impatiently for on each trip.

Helene regularly sent, every month, money to her father and her sister, with a short letter, always promising a longer one next time.

In fact, in spite of the affection she felt for them, once they had exchanged news about the weather and their health, Helene did not know what else to write about. Her life was so different from theirs. She had not been back to the island for three years as she was trying to save to pay for her Paris apartment. Next summer, she was thinking of taking Ousmane with her, to introduce him to the family. Helene had not told her parents about her plans for marriage. She preferred to tell them afterwards, to avoid questions and comments. After her experience with Hector, she had vowed never to marry and she herself was surprised at her recent decision to marry Ousmane. She was trying to get used to the idea that it was wise to settle down at last. She still had ten days to think about it before the fateful 'yes'. Lots of things could happen between now and then. Helen, being a practical woman, had seen the notary and had had a contract drawn up establishing separate property rights before and after marriage. Ousmane did not know yet, it was the gift she would give him when he got back the following day.

Ousmane, who was sincere in his love for Helene, wanted to marry her with no other motives. Gentle and shy, he was an only son; his mother came from a catholic family. His father had died a few years before, leving two other younger widows and a great many children. Ousmane rarely saw his half-brothers and sisters, neither did he visit his mother's family, who had not approved of the marriage of their daughter to a Moslem, all the more so as she had left the church.

Before he met Helene, Ousmane's whole life had been his mother. Now, he was genuinely overshadowed by his wife-to-be, who thought and decided for him. With her, he felt secure. He did not like making decisions. As a child, he had always obeyed his mother, at school, he followed the example of others more clever than he was and it had not bothered him. In his professional life he was a good assistant who methodically carried out his boss's orders. Well-thought of, he had no aspirations to be in charge. His mother would have preferred him to marry a local girl; but all those whom he had approached had fleeced him on their first date. He had to deck them out from head to toe, his modest salary did not last a week. And he could not think of marrying a girl from just any background without difficulty. The caste to which he belonged was considered inferior. Helene, on the other hand, not only demanded nothing of him, but sometimes insisted on paying in his stead, and she was the one who gave him presents. Ousmane thought that beneath her appearance of an emancipated, difficult woman, Helene had a kind, generous heart and hoped to win her over totally.

Reading her compatriot's diary made Helene more determined than ever. She was ready to avenge her. She wanted to make every man on earth suffer, to humiliate all men, to emasculate them. With the help of the whisky, she was beginning to get angry; she no longer knew how far she had got. The ash-tray was overflowing, the smoke-filled air enveloped her in an unhealthy fog that it was impossible to breathe and which made her eyes and her ideas blurry. She felt sick and automatically went to open the bay-window. The cool, damp, February air did her good and made the air in the room more healthy. She tipped the contents of the ashtray through the window and poured herself a double whisky.

Helene did not know how much she had had to drink; it was not important. It was good to be a little drunk. Since she had started going out with Ousmane in fact, she had thought herself always too clear-headed, because he did not smoke and only drank Coca-Cola. Helene had cut down on her excessive consumption of alcohol and cigarettes. Ousmane had not asked her to, but, once, he said to her very gently 'I don't think tobacco and alcohol are good for one's health ...'

Helene got up again and put on a record. It was a singer from home; he sang about love and the beautiful girls from the islands, with a touch of humour typical of her homeland. Helene smiled and went back to her story.

Saturday, August 26, 1961

It is three o'clock in the afternoon, I am back with my diary. Since morning I feel calm and serene, even a little happy. Writing does me good, I think, for once, I have something to

46

keep me occupied. I offered to help Awa to pick the rice, I hummed and laughed with Diary, I teased Alioune. I haven't seen Ndeye all morning. The weather is relatively fine after the stormy night we had. Lightning struck a suburb nearby, a neighbour told Awa. Mamadou is going to the match. I hear his old 203 missing, he always has trouble starting it. If he had not married Ndeye two years ago he could have bought a new car. She costs him a fortune: *boubous*, jewels, movies, night-clubs; not to mention the money she generously dispenses at baptisms, marriages and all sorts of gatherings. Her life-style is no secret to anyone. I hear all these things on days when she sits in the courtyard under my window with her friends. Nevertheless there are attenuating circumstances: they don't know how much their husbands earn. Ndeye behaves as if Mamadou were the director of the bank. Mamadou spends his salary at least a month in advance in order to keep up the appearance of a grand *seigneur*.

Look! Here they come, preceded by the little servant girl who is barely fifteen and who slaves under Ndeye's strict supervision for less than three thousand francs per month. She is struggling bravely under the weight of an armchair twice her size. She will have to make two more trips because the 'three Graces', Ndeye, Binta and Astou, will not lift a finger to help her. Astou is taller than the other two, who are however both extra-ordinarily hefty. She looks as if she is wearing her entire jewellery box. She must be carrying around on her person at least a pound of gold today: her earrings are so heavy that to keep them on they have to be attached by a black thread tied around her ears so that the ear-lobes won't tear. Around her neck she is wearing a huge Agadés cross. (This cross must be the latest fashion because all three of them are wearing one.) On her left wrist, she has a watch, gold of course, seven little gold bangles, one for each day of the week, and a bracelet made of gold coins which jingle. Her fat, podgy, fingers are loaded with fancy, filigree rings. On her right arm, a bracelet, a good ten centimetres thick, in the shape of a mask. Where does all that gold come from? Either jewels bought on credit, borrowed, gifts from their husbands, or, a great deal of them, gifts received in exchange for favours rendered to a wealthy and generous gentlemen ...

In a minute Ndeye will send the little servant girl to buy beer, then they will gossip maliciously about all the households in the neighbourhood and about the other women they know. There is one thing which astonishes me, these three *diriankées* (Awa's word for them) are the best of friends; yet, let one of them leave the others for a moment and the other two don't hestitate to make nasty and barbed remarks behind her back. Whenever Binta comes alone, for example, the topic of conversation is often Astou's extravagance towards a certain Sherif, whose beloved and unfaithful fourth wife she means to become. Meanwhile Binta is in search of a permanent liaison since her husband abandoned her for a young wife, a pretty and well-groomed mid-wife. He hardly comes to see her any more. At the end of the month, he sends her allowance and the usual sack of rice by his chauffeur. Today I don't feel like listening to their litany of calumnies, for I want to keep my good humour. So I am going to take advantage of the opportunity to listen to a record in the drawing room.

By some miracle, I had managed to keep a few records of classical music well hidden in the bottom of my wardrobe. Ndeye does not like this kind of music. I know what would become of my records if they fell into her hands. Music is the one thing which can still move me, make me feel alive again, take me away from the indifference of the world which surrounds me. It is like a breath of fresh air which soothes and uplifts at the same time, which makes me smile or weep.

I can't make up my mind between Beethoven's 'Ninth Symphony' and 'Adagio' by Albinoni. I choose the Ninth, because I know that listening to the Adagio, a real hymn of love, will depress me; whereas the final chorus of the Ninth, generally, fills me with hope. For a few moments, I can dream that I am young and beautiful, that the future belongs to me.

Sunday, August 27, 1961, 7 a.m.

Opening my window this morning, I am greeted by a gloomy, grey sky. The immense sadness mingled with rage which has kept me awake all night is in tune with the weather. As far back as I can remember, I cannot think of any wrong-doing on my part grievous enough to merit this life of expiation. I have made up my mind not to accept my fate as the will of God any longer, I want to overcome it. I will no longer turn the other cheek. I will no longer return good for evil. I will direct my revolt against my enemies!

The courtyard is deserted. The mango tree, beautiful and lush, seems to taunt me with the splendour of its foliage, washed clean by the rains. It is the rainy season. I am going to write about the present now. My past is so far away and so uneventful.

Up until now, Ndeye, was of no interest to me, I disdained her silently. Recently, I feel differently about her, more determined, more strongly.

Yesterday I was listening to Beethoven's 'Ninth Symphony' in the drawing-room, taking advantage of a time when she is in the yard with her friends because the drawing-room is too hot. As the record reached the last chorus I turned up the volume to drown out the *pachanga* that they were listening to on the radio, in the yard. Also, I felt a deep desire to lose myself entirely in the music. My eyes closed, I was lost in 'The Hymn of Joy' when Ndeye came into the drawing-room. Furious, she took off the record, broke it and then slapped my face, yelling about my 'crazy music'. I had never hit anyone, no one had ever struck me, except once when I was six or seven: my father slapped me because I had broken

49

my gold chain while I was undressing. The chain had caught on my dress. I felt the same astonishment in the face of this unnecessary outburst of violence. I was too surprised to react. I sat for a long time in my armchair, unable to rouse myself. It was the first time that she had dared to hit me. Awa took her side, at least partly; she told her:

'You did the right thing. She tires our ears, with her music; but you did not need to hit her.'

'Yes, poor, harmless creature, you must not hit her,' added Binta, 'you will make her spiteful.'

'Just let her show her spite and I will fix her business once and for all. There will be one less useless mouth to feed,' Ndeye replied.

Right now I have not yet decided on anything definite. But, although I am not inclined to violence, I cannot just accept that slap in the face. If I do not retaliate Ndeye will quickly make it a habit to hit me whenever she feels like. Until now she was satisfied to make vague threats.

Binta does not know just how right she is: I am going to become more than spiteful. Ndeye will pay very dearly for the two years of insults that I have just been through in her presence without saying a word in reply. That slap in the face was the last drop that made my cup of passivity overflow and transformed my patience into a raging torrent.

3.00 p.m.

I have not eaten since morning as I did not want to find myself sitting face to face with my 'enemies' over the midday meal. As soon as the meal was finished, Ndeye hastened to give what was left to two young *talibés*, to ensure that I could not come and eat later, as I sometimes do. The house is calm. It is the sacred hour of the Sunday afternoon siesta. Awa is dozing on a mat, under the mango tree, with two of the children. Diary must have gone out.

I had not written anything for a very long time and I am so

pleased that I remember some grammatical rules which I'd thought I'd long forgotten. I allow myself to be captivated by the magic of the words, I concentrate on forming my letters. Still, it is a very strange idea which I've had these last few days, to write the story of my life. But it is one way to keep myself occupied and perhaps it is good therapy for my anxieties. Already I feel more secure. I am sure there are things about the past which escape me. It is such a long time since I've been silent, indifferent to people and to things. Today my only certainty is having come to life again. I listen to my heart beating excitedly, and my blood rushing through my veins. I am painfully aware of a need for tenderness, my young body cries out, perhaps hopes for tomorrow.

I waited for Mamadou this morning at about eleven o'clock, when he was labouring over his starter in the car. Ndeye was still lolling about in her room. I had not spoken to him for two years.

'Ndeye broke my Beethoven record and she boxed me. You can't do anything about the box, but can you buy me another record? You know how important that music is in my life.'

I delivered my speech in one breath, stealing a glance at him. He looked at me with intensity; astonishment written all over his handsome face. I thought I saw a certain weariness in his eyes. He shook his head, pressed harder on the starter. The motor turned over. Without looking at me this time he said:

'I am really sorry. I haven't got a franc on me, I owe a lot of money. I would rather not hear about your household arguments.'

Then he drove off. I watched the car as it drove away and turned right on to the main road; then I went back to my room, determined to take my revenge. Because, in spite of his debts, yesterday evening, as he did every Saturday, he had taken Ndeye to the cinema and then to a night club. It was probably four o'clock this morning when I heard them come

51

in. Awa never goes out on Saturday. Saturday evenings are specially reserved for Ndeye, the official wife. The only presentable wife, because Awa is illiterate and not educated in the European sense, and because I am crazy and irresponsible.

And yet Ndeye, the favoured one, the modern, intellectual woman, is not really very educated beneath her veneer of superficial knowledge. She managed to get the coveted certificate at the end of the primary school by copying from Binta, her neighbour, so they say. Since then, she picks up all her culture from magazines and all-in-picture romances for European shop-girls. Lately she has decided to put her knowledge to the service of her country, by looking for a job as a secretary-typist in a government office. She is learning to type on an ancient machine, a legacy from the former colonial power, kept back from an inventory and given to her as a long term loan by a gentleman who had also promised her a job in his office. At the moment the passages she is typing have as many mistakes as words. I hope they will hire her without giving her a test first, for that would be detrimental.

As I am thinking of the 'lady', here she comes. Her *pagne* knotted around her, her towel over her shoulder, madame is going to perform her ablutions, then dressed like a queen, she will accompany Mamadou on a visit to one of their friends. Unless there is a baptism, for she never misses one. I wonder if she is really invited to all these gatherings? Sometimes by chance a friend comes by in the morning and tells her: 'So and so is having a baptism today', and immediately she drapes herself in one of her enormous ceremonial *boubous* and goes off with her friend, even if she had something else planned for that day. How could Mamadou have taken a woman like that under his roof?

I look at Awa, sitting in the yard. She has taken off her head-tie to re-tie it, her gestures are graceful. Her hair is braided in the shape of a pineapple towards the top of her head, and adorned with two charms. Several little gold rings hang from her ears.

She has fine regular features, healthy, black skin which has never been exposed to cheap creams and powders, hands with fine tapered fingers. On the ring-finger of her left hand she wears a simple band of plaited copper. She is well proportioned, fairly tall. She is beautiful without artifice. I have never felt the least resentment towards Awa. I can't understand why she approved of Ndeye's attitude yesterday. Normally she does not interfere in quarrels which don't concern her.

Diary has just come in with two school friends. They seem particularly exuberant, I think they are coming back from the cinema. It must have been an Indian film: one of the girls demonstrates a dance for Awa. All three are talking at once, trying to tell the story or at least what they understood of it. Diary has brought peanuts for her brothers. She always brings them something when she goes out.

Mamadou and Ndeye, richly bedecked, cross the courtyard. They go out without a glance in my direction, greeting Awa as they go. The sun goes off towards other mornings. I put down notebook and pencil until tomorrow, and close my window before the mosquitoes come.

Monday, August 28, 1961

After a relatively sleepless night, I was awakened before dawn by a veritable howling which tore me from the nightmare in which I was struggling: in my dream four masked men, with naked hairy bodies, grinning and taunting me in a language I didn't understand, were pulling my arms and legs. Between each cry I heard the voice of the *muezzin* calling the faithful to the *fajar* morning prayer. Soon I recognised Awa's voice, Mamadou's hurried steps and Ndeye's running as they crossed the drawing-room and went towards Awa's room, which was next to mine. I got up and opened my window. The leafy branches of the mango tree shone with particular brilliance against the pearly grey of the early dawn. I left my room and went to see what was happening.

Awa came out, tearing her hair, rolling on the ground, Ndeye trying to hold her up, to calm her. When I got to Awa's room, I saw the three children: Diary huddled up against the wall; Oulimata with his back to his sister in the same bed, his eyes open, lifeless; Alioune, lying on his back, legs apart and his arms folded. His face was a beautiful smiling mask: nose pinched, thin-lipped, his mouth slightly open. Mamadou seemed to have aged ten years. He did not even look up when I entered. I put my hand on his shoulder in a gesture of affection. He took hold of it and, squeezing my fingers, thanked me.

I went back to my room and locked myself in. Hidden behind my shutters, I could watch what was happening through the openings. The nearest neighbours were the first to arrive; then the courtyard was quickly invaded by curious passers-by, in search of news to fill their conversations. The uncles and aunts from Thirty-third Street arrived very soon. A horse-drawn carriage brought about fifty chairs, which were set around the courtyard, under my window as well. The crowd overflowed through the open gate onto the sidewalk. A fire-brigade ambulance took away the bodies. About mid-day they served great bowls of rice. Those who had not gone home were chatting away as happily as at a baptism.

Numerous theories were advanced as to what had caused the children's sudden death: they spoke of worms which suffocate children as they sleep; of the *ounk* which contaminates food and causes poisoning; of powder which curdles the milk; of the neighbour's evil eye and even of the co-wife, in this case Ndeye, since I did not count. Some people, happy at meeting an old friend, were talking about something quite different, enquiring about relatives and friends, talking about work, commenting on the difficulties of modern life.

About three o'clock the men set off for the burial. The women told their beads or spoke to each other in low voices.

A man monotonously chanted verses from the Koran.

Awa, on a mat under the mango tree, surrounded by the women in the family, had a permanent look of astonishment on her face. From time to time a tear would well up in her beautiful eyes which seemed bigger than ever.

At last the men came back from the cemetery. They brought the three *pagnes* which had covered the children's bodies. Then Awa broke into a long wailing which made me shudder. In spite of everything I understood her sorrow, I, who had not seen my child born, I, who would never give birth to a child, a barren tree, forgotten by everyone, whose solitude not a single soul came to trouble that day.

It is getting darker, I cannot write any more. Such is life. One day the breath of life takes flight on the wings of a gentle breeze, in the dawn of a quiet morning, and no one can foresee this end. If one day man unravels this mystery he will be like God, and our world will have no more reason to exist. We need this permanently threatening us, to remind us that beyond man there exists an absolute power. Rich, poor, great and small, we are all condemned men and women, temporarily reprieved. Until tomorrow then and perhaps a new reprieve.

The annoying squeak of the record player forced Helene to get up to change the record. She put on Beethoven's Ninth in memory of this young woman who had come to suffer on African soil an exile more horrible than that she had known in Europe. The strange death of the children remained a mystery to her. She had read the news item in the local daily papers which she had delivered to her Paris address in the holidays. One often heard about the sudden deaths of children, which could be explained by malnutrition and inadequate hygiene which caused the slightest infection to be fatal. But three from the same family and at the same time...

A few days before, Helene had brought to the hospital the body of a little boy who, according to his mother, had been playing normally the day before. The mother seeing that he had a high fever and that his eyes were staring, brought him to the clinic. As she considered his condition to be serious, the mid-wife who had examined him had asked Helene to go with the sick boy to the hospital. Before they reached the hospital, the child died, without anyone being able to determine the cause of death. He was buried a few hours later. The family had not sought to find out what had caused his death. It was the will of Allah, Allah had taken him. The natural or supernatural causes of the death mattered little as a result. Helene had forgotten the diagnosis put forward. She always had a feeling of powerless rebellion when a child died in her care. In spite of almost twenty years in her profession, she could not really get used to the suffering of others. The whisky, the cigarettes, the wild parties were a way of arming herself against pity, of doing her work without exposing her own feelings of compassion.

Had she begun reading this diary at an opportune moment? She felt in some confused way that reading it was going to change her life. She was at an important crossroads. For the first time for years, she had, of her own accord, stopped rushing around, trying to gain time. Just to read a true story. To reflect, to look back, to question her usual attitude. And she was discovering that her life was very empty. She had deliberately closed her heart to love, to compassion, for fear of the suffering it might bring her, and as a result she was living a marginal existence. When she had met Ousmane, guessing how shy he was, she had decided to seduce him to amuse herself.

Jacques had given a Christmas party at his place. Among the usual crowd, heavy drinkers and carousers, Ousmane stood out, the only one drinking Coca-Cola. Jacques responded to Helene's amazement by introducing her to Ousmane. She had taken his arm forcibly, to make him dance with her. She had so rubbed herself against him that at the end of the piece, Ousmane was ready to pounce on her. She kept him breathless for the whole evening, then at dawn she disappeared. She was not very far away, she was in Jacques' bed.

Ousmane, who thought she had left, asked for her address and rushed round to her house. When she got home, two or three hours later, she found him outside her door. She let him in, made him have a shower and then put him to bed. Ousmane's behaviour towards Helene was like that of a good little boy; he had not even tried to kiss her. Since she wanted him to go to sleep, he closed his eyes and, tired from his sleepless night, he fell asleep. Helene worked on some files which she always

56

brought home, then went to join him. As she pulled aside the screen which hid the bed, he woke up.

'I am sorry, I didn't really mean to fall asleep...'

She looked at hime like someone about to consume a tasty morsel. He felt paralysed by the way she looked at him. He had never met such a fascinating woman. She slowly untied the knot which held her négligé, which spread out around her like an enchantment. She replied in a deep voice which was no more than a whisper: 'Don't say you are sorry.'

Ousmane told himself that he should do something, get up, take her in his arms, kiss her. Still he remained stock-still, rooted to the bed, all his muscles, tense and aching. She took an eternity to cross the two metres which separated them, in short, she took all the initiatives.

When he left her, his mind was made up: this woman had left his brain in a whirl and he had to have her; so he would marry her. He asked Jacques about her. She was single and unattached. Two days later, he asked her for her hand, which made her laugh until tears ran down her cheeks. She thought him weird, charming. She told him that if she had wanted to get married, she had already had dozens of opportunities. Then he answered tenderly:

'You need one thing more to be really fulfilled as a woman. I can give you this one little thing: a child who will give your life a purpose.'

'You really think so?'

She stopped laughing. He had touched a chord in her, deeper that he could have imagined. For some time Helene had felt the desire to have a child of her own. She had already thought of taking one of her many nieces or nephews to live with her, but this solution did not fully satisfy her.

After thinking about it for a few days, she decided to marry Ousmane. Physically, she was attracted to him, and he was gentle by nature. She was sure to dominate him, so she was not taking a big risk. At the first sign of trouble, she would ask for a divorce; this way out would always be there.

Helene's throat was dry from smoking. She knew she had drunk and smoked enough and that she should go to bed. Nevertheless she decided to read the whole notebook through to the very end. She took another mouthful of scotch, closed her eyes to be swallowed up as well in the *final chorus of Beethoven's 'Ninth Symphony'. She had never before listened to it which such pleasure; she could understand just how comforting the 'Hymn to Joy' could be to this young woman, alone in a world which she scarcely understood. Helene felt herself carried away like a straw in the wind; her whole being vibrated. When the record ended, she turned off the record-player and began to read.*

Tuesday, August 29, 1961

This morning I could not open my window to the breaking dawn, as I usually do, I could not look at the sky, breathe in the first breath of cool air before the day's dry heat. The house is still full of visitors. The relatives from the village came yesterday evening, after the *guéwé*. I saw Mamadou's mother and two of Awa's sisters. Ndeye's family was there too, in force. Very late last night I slipped into the kitchen and stocked up for today with a bottle of water and a bit of bread. The semi-darkness of my room and all the bustle outside make it difficult for me to write. I feel like staying in bed, and not thinking. A thousand thoughts of all kinds assail me, from the most disjointed to the most serious: Where do we go after death? Where are the children? Is there really a heaven, a hell, a purgatory? There is a supreme being over us, that I believe. But why is it that on this earth some people have such a good life, while others suffer only misfortune despite the fact that they are upright and honest? And if these are the same people who have the highest place in the next world, we will really have been fooled. Who has the truth? In each religion, there are fanatics who think they are the only ones who possess the key to knowledge and that everyone else is in error, that they will not be touched by God's grace...

Have I become a being without a soul? I am rambling aimlessly. The children's death, after the first moments of surprise, leaves me relatively unmoved. I don't suffer from not seeing them. Perhaps I have not yet realised that they are gone forever... Today, my faithful companions and only

58

friends, the cockroaches, take advantage of the un-natural
night in my room, they crawl all over the walls, fly about the
room, roam around my bedside table, greet each other on my
bread, their antennae bumping into each other. A bold
fellow steals a quick kiss from me and escapes above the
wardrobe. I doze, lulled by the hum of voices in the yard. I
am dreaming. Alioune is calling me 'mother'; for the first
time I am 'mother'. I open my eyes. I am all alone with my
cockroaches. Alioune is dead and I am not a mother.

Wednesday, August 30, 1961, 2 p.m.

Early this morning, before the call to prayer, I took
advantage of a fine drizzle to go to the kitchen. Some
left-over couscous allowed me to appease my hunger. After a
quick shower I went back to my room without being seen.
Two people wrapped up in their *pagnes* were snoring under
the mango tree, oblivious of the rain which wasn't really
heavy enough to penetrate the tree's abundant foliage. Soon
after the time of the morning prayer I heard a gentle
knocking at my door. I opened it a little.

'Mamadou!' My surprise was without bounds. His
reddened eyes had lost their usual glint of malice and looked
profoundly grave.

'Shhh!... I know that you are not going to venture out
with all this coming and going. I've brought you something
to eat.'

'Thank you ...'

I take the package. Was it possible, he is suddenly
thinking of me! The death of the children has made him
sensitive to the suffering of others. I ask how Awa is and close
my door quickly. His answer comes to me through the wood.

'She is brave ...'

Actually, I could not share their sorrow. I was content to
understand, to imagine their suffering. My heart is weary,
my tears too long since dried up. It is the third day. The
crowd is even larger and the din deafening, the food

plentiful. Some, it seems, have not eaten for days, judging by their voracious appetites. A young man who was eating directly beneath my window asked if it was a baptism. He was not from the neighbourhood. Passing by, he had seen the huge bowls of food and had stopped to partake. On the whole the *boubous* seemed more sombre but the jewellery was no less dazzling. I am going to have to tell Mamadou that if I die while I am under his roof he need not feed everyone for the occasion; I have more frequently abstained and fasted than feasted in my life time. Besides I will only need a simple grave, in a corner of the cemetery, with no cross or headstone, since I am already forgotten. Still it is strange to know that when I die, no one will shed a tear, for I have already ceased to exist. I am a rudderless boat adrift in time and space. Is it because I was conceived accidentally one day in Lent?

An appropriate tune comes to mind. I have forgotten the words. I make up others that are in keeping with my situation:

> *I am frustrated, depressed,*
> *I have no home,*
> *I am an exile, an alien,*
> *They say I've lost my mind.*
> *I am a wreck, drifting in the wind,*
> *I have lost all my illusions.*

Thursday, August 31, 1961

It was still dark when I woke up, bathed in sweat, my heart beating fast, surprised to find that I was not in the bottom of the pit where, asleep, I had been lying motionless, my whole body crawling with worms which devoured me. I could not see them anymore, I felt them, they had left me paralysed. I was awaiting the very last moment, the moment when the mind falls into nothingness, when my eyes opened to the solitude of my room. I was still there lying on my miserable bed.

60

I could not bear the heat and the darkness any longer so I decided to go for a walk. Once outside, I managed to open the gate noiselessly. I walked as far as the site of a set of apartment buildings being constructed in our area without meeting a single soul. Coming back, when I got to about five hundred metres from the house, I realised I was bathed in perspiration, out of breath, my heart was pounding and my legs trembling. I had not walked so far for years. The muezzin's first call gave me wings: I wanted to get back before the household woke up. Limping along as fast as I could, I barely had time to slip into the shower when I heard the drawing room door open. I stood under the shower, fully dressed, and rubbed my aching feet, then I crossed the courtyard with my head down, careless of the eyes fixed on me. I thought I saw someone praying but I couldn't tell who... Probably one of the relatives from the village who had arrived the other evening. Nobody bothered about me, nobody came to greet me. Besides, that morning they had gone off again with Awa.

I did not understand why Awa had gone. I felt more frustrated and lonely than ever before. Awa and the children had been the only ones in the house to whom I spoke... At last all is quiet again. I can open my window for a little while. It must be three o'clock. I don't think there will be any visitors before this evening. Mamadou has gone to work; Ndeye left the house when he did. The little servant girl is humming as she tackles an impressive pile of dirty laundry that must be washed before nightfall. Aunt Khady, seated on a mat, is telling her beads, mumbling her verses from the Koran. She is saying her afternoon prayers, *tisbaar*. She reminds me of Awa, whom I watched, five times a day, for almost four years, in the same spot, praising Allah. The silence and the emptiness around me weigh even more heavily now because of the crowd these past three days.

Her prayer finished, I cough to attract Aunt's attention. She smiles at me. She has always been good to me. I wave to her and ask her the question I have been burning to ask all morning.

'Why did the family take Awa away?'

'To comfort her, to try to take her mind off things. She has no one here. You are ill; Ndeye is not good for her; Mamadou is a man ...'

'Do they know what caused the children's death?'

'It is Allah's will. He gives us children and he takes them back when he needs them. We must respect his will.'

This fatalism has always amazed me. I know that in this particular case, Allah is not the only one involved ... And what about my madness, whose will was that? That is, if I could be considered mad. For the moment I am neither the mad woman of the village nor the neighbourhood. My madness is the private property of Mamadou Moustapha's house and in particular of Ndeye, his favourite and third wife. This beloved Ndeye loses nothing by waiting. I am preparing my vengeance like a very special dish. After I have carefully prepared it, seasoned it, I will savour it slowly, very slowly and carefully. It will be my last meal and my madness will vanish.

Friday, September 1, 1961

I glance briefly at the sky – hung with thick cloud, the sign of welcome showers to come – and recite my evening prayers, then my eyes fall on Mamadou. Mamadou bending low, arms raised, his face serene with the calm of his newly recovered faith. It's the first time I have seen him like this.

'Happy the man who believes in God, he will be comforted.' I note with satisfaction that Mamadou's atheism and his whisky have not survived the test ... After his prayer is finished, he comes over to my window.

'Good evening my love.'

My mouth drops open with astonishment, I pinch myself to see if I am dreaming. I must be dreaming. That is what he used to call me at the very beginning of our marriage. That

62

was so long ago! Even my name, Juletane, because my father's name was Jules, is a distant memory. No one had called me by name for years. I am 'the mad woman'.

'Yes, you are the one I turn to in my distress. I did not know before what the suffering, the misfortune of losing what is dearest was like. Up until now my life was full, this is the first time that I am so painfully aware of my powerlessness. Now I understand just how much I hurt you by abandoning you to your suffering. I hope that one day you'll forgive me. What can I do so that you will forgive me?'

'Nothing ... I don't want anything ... Or if ... Give up Ndeye, she is the source of all your troubles ... That is all I want. You are my only family, Awa is not a bad soul ...'

My reply took him by surprise, that was plain. He did not say anything, but went off, with his brand new prayer rug under his arm.

Ndeye too seemed to have got a serious shock. She did not shout at the little servant girl as she usually did; she did not look at me in her cruel, disdainful way; she did not even look in the direction of my window. She prepared the meal with one of her sisters, sent for me at lunch time and, around the bowl she ate in silence and got up with difficulty, sighing.

Mamadou had his midday meal in the drawing-room with some friends. Then they went to the mosque to take part in Friday prayer. God is great. There is only one God and Mohammed is his prophet ...

All my thoughts are with my sister Awa. Do I miss her? It is true that we could have been one big, happy family. But for that to be, I would also have to come from a little village in the bush, have been brought up in a polygamous family, taught to share my master with other women. Whereas, in fact I belong nowhere and I had dreamed of a prince charming who would be faithful and mine alone. He was to be all mine and I all his and our union would be as solid as a fortress built on a rock. But, at the first storm, I found myself at the bottom of a lonely chasm, floundering in the mire. True, life is composed of joy and sorrow, laughter and tears.

63

But mine is nothing but tears of blood. Can I live long enough to see the fatal fall of this house where my last illusions dwelled?

The day is at its hottest. Evening will surely bring a great number of visitors and confine me to my room. So I am putting down my notebook to go and have a refreshing shower.

7.00 p.m.

As I had foreseen, the stream of visitors has begun. It is not the huge crowd of the previous days. Just one or two people coming and going every five minutes. Mamadou is in the drawing-room receiving condolences. Awa, the first three days, had preferred to remain in her usual place under the mango tree across from my window. I was able to watch events unfolding. Each person would arrive, saying *Siggil ndiggaale* by way of greeting, and the whole family answered in chorus *Siggil sa wall*. Today, I can only see figures going from the gate to the drawing room and leaving again a few minutes later.

All the faces of the visitors have the same hesitant expression when they arrive; then, as they are leaving, a look of satisfaction at having done their duty, some sigh or say 'alas' which is more like a sort of entreaty than a lament. My window is half-open, but no one looks in my direction. The little servant, for once apparently idle, standing outside the kitchen door, echoes the greetings as visitors come and go.

Saturday, September 2, 1961

I am in the Palace Theatre, it is a gala evening. The show is a lively French cancan and everybody is appreciative of the dancers' lacy underwear. Mamadou gets up to applaud and the room is transformed into a supermarket. I pick up a basket to do my shopping, remember that I have no money and let go of the metal basket. The noise it makes as it falls mingles with the gate opening ... The applause was someone knocking at the door. An unfamiliar voice, then Mamadou's and the noise of footsteps disturb my dream and bring me back to the reality of a day dawning. I open my window. One of Awa's young brothers is standing under the mango tree beside Mamadou.

'What is going on?'

'Awa threw herself into the well in our field last night,' replies Oumar, Awa's brother.

'Troubles never come singly,' I murmur, more for myself than for anyone else.

Mamadou looks at me questioningly and despairingly. He cannot understand what is happening to him: to lose his three children and his first wife in less than a week ...

Life is a wheel of fortune, it keeps turning and no one knows when it will stop. If a man weeps, weep with him, for if you laugh, your laughter can change into wailing the next time the wheel stops. And so others will laugh at you ... I understand others' grief, but, oh God, forgive me for not mingling my tears with Mamadou's. I have so often wept alone because of him.

The day runs its course, a long reel of boredom. The house has lost its customary animation. No shouts from the children, no more Awa, busy between the mango tree and the kitchen. The little maid does not hum to the rhythm of her broom as she sweeps the corners of the courtyard. Mamadou is gone to the village with Oumar, Awa's young brother. The family from Thirty-third Street, Ndeye's sisters and most of Mamadou's friends have probably gone as well. A few visitors, mainly women who have heard the news, come by to see Ndeye. Binta and Astou came at about three o'clock, but didn't stay long, they were on their way to a christening. So, between Awa's death and the various ceremonies of a Saturday in town, the family and friends of the household are all busy. Ndeye has no choice, by force of circumstances, but to be alone with me.

Today, no armchair under my window, no beer, no

pachanga, no movies this evening either and no night-clubbing afterwards. A very austere life for Ndeye. She is wearing a dark *boubou* and considerably less jewellery. However, she is still wearing her startling make-up: instead of eyebrows, two bold pencil lines which disappear into the wig she wears for special occasions. I have always wondered where this fashion came from – Ndeye was not the only one who followed it, but her wigs were each more bizarrely shaped than the last; as for the material, it was easy to see the artificial strands of fibre which took the place of her hair ...

Ndeye seems very preoccupied. I don't think Awa's death is the only reason for her distress, although her future as favourite wife is seriously in jeopardy, because she has no children. Mamadou will take another wife, a younger one, and she will lose her privileges. But the fact that she cannot go to parade her jewels at some baptism must really bother her ... If I continue to feel sorry for her, I run the risk of weeping over the plight of poor Ndeye, while the hour of my vengeance is approaching. Besides, I have run out of tears. I have discovered hatred and this feeling drives me as much as my love did in the past.

Yes, I was once beautiful, in love. Today I looked at myself in a broken bit of mirror, my hair, which I had cut, never seems to have grown back – or did I cut it again recently? It is dusty and dull. There is a long diagonal scar across my forehead, a souvenir of my first depression, on the third weekend Mamadou spent in the village with Awa. I thought that the world had stopped that weekend, that a future without Mamadou's faithful and exclusive love was inconceivable. My eyes, too shiny, have a cold, disturbing look about them; my cheek-bones stand out above the hollows of my cheeks; my skin is without lustre. I look desperate, starved. Not of bread, but of someone's presence, of tenderness, of gentle caresses. Oh God! What has become of the smiling, happy woman I used to be? Five years have passed; five years of humiliation, of indifference, of being disdained by others. Such has been the lot of this stranger, all alone in the world, that I am. I am very lucid now. Have I reached the end of the Calvary which has been my life in this country?

6.30 p.m.

The wind is blowing through the mango-tree, it is incredibly violent, I hope it will blow away the mosquitoes. It will certainly rain tonight.

The courtyard is deserted. Ndeye must be in her room or in the kitchen with the maid. She will have the evening meal by herself. I would not want to find myself alone with her. Besides, I don't trust what she might make me swallow. I believe her capable of anything …

I had become accustomed to a certain monotonous daily rhythm with Awa and the children as my link with the outside world. Now that they are gone a new threshold has been crossed. Living with Mamadou and Ndeye, even provisionally, would be unbearable. I have to find a solution once and for all, and as soon as possible. Ndeye is the stumbling block on the already tortuous path of my life. I must remove this obstacle so that I can see clearly. And then, as I could before, I will be able to face the future with excitement, and say to myself 'Tomorrow is another day'.

Sunday, September 3, 1961

The night is calm; it is still dark, the muezzin has not yet called the faithful to prayer. Too many things are whirling about in my head. I feel a bit feverish, it is probably the heat. The rain which was threatening yesterday did not fall. I have taken the bulb from the shower to replace the one in my room which had burnt out. I should have thought of it sooner. At last I can write without opening my window, and especially without having to wait for it to be light. Awa's death is in the natural course of things, although I did not expect it. I realise that I underestimated her; I did not think she was

67

capable of so much determination and courage. It is much easier to take another's life than to do away with oneself. If there is the slightest glimmer of hope buried in the depth of your being, you can overcome the greatest difficulties. She could have had other children. She was the only one in the house who prayed and respected the teachings of Islam. But alas! her faith was not sufficient to surmount the cruel ordeal.

What surprises me most of all was the fact that the children's death should be accepted with so much fatalism by the rest of the family. Allah wanted them, Allah had taken them, Aunt had told me. No autopsy, no police enquiry. Unless they had taken place without my knowing ...

My throat is dry, my head burning. I go to the kitchen and open the refrigerator. My nostrils are suddenly assailed by the odour characteristic of the mixture of all the different sauces stored there, in spite of the piece of coal they had put there, which, they say, absorbs odours. This piece of coal, I must admit, has been there for some time and could hardly absorb anything now. I drink from the bottle. I don't normally do that. But I want to do something different from my normal routine ...

I notice a knife, a long, beautiful knife that Mamadou had bought at the last *tabaski* festival, for sacrificing the sheep. Mamadou is a good Moslem, he is polygamous and he celebrates *tabaski*.

On that day, he goes to the mosque, kills his sheep, distributes a great deal of meat and what is left is transformed into delicious kebabs which he enjoys marinaded with the best wines. In short, he respects the least restrictive aspects of Islam. During the Ramadan he cannot fast, because his stomach ulcer, conveniently, obliges him to eat regularly ...

As if hypnotised, I take the knife. The tip is very pointed. In a corner of the courtyard I rub the blade on a stone which has often been used for this purpose. I go to Ndeye's room; she is sleeping soundly, as always. I wait until my eyes get used to the darkness. She is lying on her right side, covered to the waist. Her ample breasts are bare and exposed. For a moment I calculate the position of her heart under the layers of fat and then I drive the knife in, with both hands. The blade goes all the way in between two ribs. Her whole body writhes convulsively ... I feel a warm liquid on my left foot. She is urinating. After what seems to me to be quite a long time, she is quite still. I remove the pillow, open the window. Her face has become a hideous death mask, her eyes are glassy. Next I go to Awa's room where Mamadou has chosen to spend the night so that he could remember his dear departed ones. I knock carefully before entering. He is lying on his back, his hands under his head.

'Good morning, sweetheart.'

'Good morning ...'

'You are surprised to see me, aren't you? Don't I have the right to visit my husband? Aren't we married for better or for worse? I have been neglected so long ...'

His look is a gentle caress on my skin, taut with impatience. I go up to the bed slowly and lean over him. He takes me in his arms.

'We can begin all over again, if you want,' says Mamadou.

In reply, I lean closer to him. I am happy. I think of Ndeye who Mamadou is going to find dead. I have my vengeance. I burst out laughing at the thought of all that beautiful red blood flowing from Ndeye's side. Ndeye, silenced at last. She won't insult me any more. What a lovely joke, Mamadou's favourite out of the running!

'Come, sweetheart, listen carefully ... No ... Nothing ...'

I cannot stop laughing, I laugh until I cry. He will soon know the extent of his misfortune. And about the children's death. Who is responsible for their death ... ? Didn't they prescribe drops for me? Drops that Mamadou himself was to make me take, and that were to be kept out of the childen's reach ... ? Of course, Mamadou had given them to me, telling me 'No more than ten drops, all right?'. At that moment, he was thinking that if I swallowed the whole bottle

I would solve my problem. This medicine could take care of other things ...

Here come the children. All three of them have come back, they have gathered around me, pulling me by the hand. We are jumping, dancing, laughing. My laughter ends in a fit of coughing. I come back to reality. I am lying flat on the dirty kitchen floor. Did I fall ... ?

The knife is still in its place ... Mamadou has gone to the village for Awa's funeral. Ndeye must still be asleep. I feel very feverish, I am lost, I am perspiring profusely. Now I am cold, freezing cold. My teeth are chattering. I light the fire to make some tea. The sight of the flame warms me. I am afraid, my head is like an enormous kettle with a thousand explosive thoughts boiling up inside. One of them suddenly flashes brightly, like a spark of magma, and soon it outshines all the others. I am feverish with excitement ... Oh happy household where nothing is ever locked, neither in the kitchen, nor in Ndeye's room. Poor Ndeye, who is sleeping like a log. Blessed Sunday when we are alone ...

I am at the bottom of the pit once more. I am no longer alone. My eyes have got used to the dark and I have found a passage which leads to a sort of gallery. Crawling along a long tunnel I reached the banks of an underground river where there was great activity but where all was silent. Men and women were bathing or sitting on rocks with their feet in the water. They all looked happy and joyful, like people who had reached a welcome rest after a long walk. No one spoke. I plunged into the water to try to wash off all the mud from the pit which clung to my skin and my clothing. I swam under water for a while. When I came up again, I had the same feeling of being cleansed and rested that I could read on the faces of the others.

'Where are we?' I asked the young woman nearest to me.

'Shhh! Not so loud, you mustn't disturb anyone. Everyone here is on an inward journey and goes wherever he wants to. Earth is only a stage which we pass through, man's body is dust. Only the spirit is inspired and divine. We wash because we have to keep the outer shell which protects the soul clean, so that no impurity will trouble our reflection. All those people gathered on the banks of the river came here, exhausted and dirty, from different far-off places. The only thing which unites them is their hypersensitivity, flayed by all the harshness and evil on the other side of the river.'

'I feel calm and rested, the water is so cool ... Can we go back one day to the other world from which we come ... ?'

'Some go back there and do not make out very well. It demands a lot of strength and courage. They are often disappointed and come back to us. Here, life is easy, you just have to let your thoughts wander and live your inner life intensely.'

'I think I would like to go back there. I don't know why, but I think there is someone I would like to see again ...'

'Well, I will leave you. Take advantage of your innermost self. Those on the other side of the river look down on us. In their launguage we are mad. Look at our friends, their faces only show wisdom and kindness.'

Someone is calling me from the other side of the river. Someone is speaking to me. I think I know this man. It is hard for me to remember how I met him. He takes my hand. I am crossing a yard that I know very well, there is a tree. We go out. He puts me into a car, very gently. He is handsome and I think he is someone I love. I ask him his name. He answers: 'I am Mamadou, don't worry, everything will be alright.'

We are crossing the town. There are lots of lights, houses with many storeys, cars, motorcycles. Sometimes the car stops and people cross. They seem to be in a great hurry. We get to a lighted sign, Mamadou brakes, leans out the window, and talks to a man in uniform who raises a barrier. The car goes slowly, makes several turns, then Mamadou shuts off the engine in front of a long building and helps me to get out. We cross a long corridor and come to a verandah.

Opposite, there is a courtyard and several cottages. A lady helps me to get into a bed in one of the cottages. Then she gives me an injection; saying it will do me good, that I will sleep …

I close my eyes, Mamadou is beside me. I am wearing a pretty white dress. A man standing behind a table in front of us, is speaking to us. He asks Mamadou a question, Mamadou says yes. Then he speaks to me. I too answer: yes. Then Mamadou takes my left hand, very tenderly. Slowly he slips a gold ring on one of my fingers (a gold ring, the symbol of unity, a pledge of love, a promise of fidelity, the assurance of happiness) then he embraces me. Other people; men, women, blacks, whites, are embracing me, talking to me. From their clear voices flow wishes, sweet as honey. I am very happy. It is the happiest day of my life, the prelude of a symphony of love which will never end.

A light mist envelops us, faces pass before my eyes and then disappear, swallowed up in the fog. Mamadou is pulling me along with him. We are waltzing, caught up in a whirlwind, and I let myself be carried along by the soothing mist. I fall asleep calmed.

Tuesday, September 5, 1961

I am in the hospital again, in a cottage. I am very calm and lucid. I found my exercise book: there are only two blank pages left. I had hidden it around my waist, under my dress. I must finish my journal, it is the only legacy I am leaving to Mamadou. I hope he will read it and will understand how far from my dream he was. The nurse looked at me just now, leafing through my notebook, I smiled at her, and, reassured, she went away …

Last Sunday I went into the kitchen. After imagining Ndeye's bloody murder while looking at the knife, I hit upon the first idea which came into my agitated brain. I poured a litre of oil into a saucepan and I heated it. The first time I thought about revenge, I thought about taking Ndeye's life. But all things considered, it was better that she continue to live, disfigured. So that as long as she lived, she could think

72

about how she had hurt me. All the more so as I had not been able to do away with her. With the knife and all that blood, I could not have done it ... Armed with my saucepan full of very hot oil, I went to the room. The door creaked, Ndeye did not budge. She was lying on her side, her face towards the wall. I wanted her full face, with her eyes open. I called her, touching her on the shoulder. When she opened her eyes, wondering what was happening, with the other hand which I had kept hidden behind my back, I poured the whole panful of oil in her face. She howled like a wounded animal and leapt out bed. It was easy to get out of her way for she could not see. I went and locked myself in my room. Ndeye groped her way to the gate. A neighbour took her to the hospital. I have not seen her again since. I hope she will live long enough to remember.

The little servant girl came in, the curious bystanders each went back home. Very few people knew that I existed. I remained in a state of nervous prostration all day long, with periods of lucidity. In the evening Mamadou and his uncle arrived; someone had told them. I remember that I told him: 'She hit me and God punished her; I did not touch her,' repeating the same words over and over. I believed what I was saying, having spent the whole day telling myself over and over again that I was innocent, that I was the victim of a fate over which I had no control. So Mamadou brought me here. They gave me an injection and I spent a peaceful night.

Yesterday my head was not very clear. A light mist enveloped everything around me; still I could make out a faint glimmer of light way above me which revealed the outline of a well. A languorous melody ran through my veins, rocking me gently, carrying me away. A sweet smell, coming from far away and long ago, reminded me of an emerald countryside. A cool, limpid stream gurgled in my ear. Then all at once I heard a call which had been resounding in my mind for years. 'Come back to your island.'

Today I am waiting for Mamadou. He will certainly come this evening. I will give him this notebook, my confidante and my witness ... There are lots of shadowy areas in my memory and things I can't explain. Did I really lose my mind at times?

I had not expected Awa's death. On Sunday the twenty-seventh at supper, we had a meal of boiled millet, prepared by Awa. She ate, then got up from the table, leaving me alone with the children. Did I pour the contents of the medicine bottle into the children's drinking-cup? Or did I leave the bottle where they could reach it? I don't remember anything ...

I had taken the bottle intending to swallow a few drops, as I sometimes did to have a quiet night. I found it empty in the pocket of my dress, the next day, the day after the children's death. I could not explain how it had got there. Perhaps it was not properly closed and spilled accidentally ... I prefer this explanation. I would not like to know I was responsible for the death of the children. I was fond of them, I did not wish them any harm. However their death had pierced Mamadou's armour of indifference.

A few years ago when we moved into our present home, Awa's house, Mamadou had the courtyard cemented. 'It will be cleaner and easier to keep than sand,' he said. In the middle, he planted a mango tree which was already fairly big. Every day Awa would water it, adding manure regularly. The mango tree grew rapidly. After two rainy seasons the foliage was already beautiful and lush and we could sit in its shade. Until today it has never borne any fruit, whereas other trees in the neighbourhood, much less healthy, have mangoes. Recently, Awa said to me that it must be a barren tree – her look said 'like you' – and that in the long run she regretted having lavished her care on it to no avail. In both cases, Mamadou had had no luck. I too was that barren tree, that tree which I saw every morning interminably. I thought that apart from the seasons nothing would ever come to alter the rhythm of our narrow little lives around the mango tree. But what can man do to halt the march of time? No one can say 'Tomorrow I will do this or I will not do that'. The memory of the entire world carved in stone or traced on fresh parchment cannot change the fact that the human heart is forgetful by nature. If my reason wandered from time to time, who is to blame? A phrase which I once read comes to mind: 'He who creates a monster of pain should not be surprised if one day he is destroyed by it'. Who said these words, where did I read them? Was I this monster of pain? I don't know. The only truth I know is that under the thick clay of the walls I have at last found the crack which allowed me to escape from the pit.

Wednesday, September 6, 1961, 4.30 p.m.

A nurse gave me a few sheets of paper so I can continue to write. Last night it rained all night. This morning when I woke up a curtain of rain hid the horizon. I could not leave my room until about nine o'clock. A few patients were walked up and down the verandah. I went to the nurses' station where a whole group of women chatted or babbled away happily, taking different medications under the watchful but benevolent eye of two nurses. One of the patients with whom I had exchanged a few words the day before followed me back to my room to chat. Her name is Oumy. Her husband, she told me, had locked her up in one room for two years and was living with another woman. They often forgot to give her anything to eat; then she would scream and knock on the door. They said she was mad and one day she was brought here. Speaks good French and seems like a very pleasant person. My knowledge of their native language is still very imprecise but I am able to exchange a few remarks with the other patients since some of them speak a little French. Some of them are accompanied by a relative. It seems to me that they are all victims of a selfish world which crushes them carelessly.

For me life here is an improvement over the solitude and hostility of these last two years in Mamadou's house. The nurses are all cheerful and kind. You can hardly distinguish

75

them from the patients and relatives because they don't wear uniforms. I am very happy to be alone in my room. It is a round hut, thatched with straw. The bed is on the left inside the entrance; on the right, under the window, are a table and two chairs. Behind a floral curtain, there is a basin and a mirror.

The doctor who came to see me yesterday is young and sympathetic. Our conversation was in no way like the interrogation I had been through in Mamadou's presence when I had seen the doctor a few years before. He asked me if I remembered when I first became ill. I couldn't answer, since I had never thought of myself as ill, which made him smile. Did I know that the children and Mamadou's first wife were dead? Yes, I knew, but I did not know what had brought about their deaths. Had I thrown hot oil on the third wife? Where that was concerned, I remembered everything. Nevertheless I said no. Since I had decided that Ndeye had never existed, I could not have attacked her.

He talked about dissemblance, of primary, secondary, chronic depression, of various medicines with difficult names. Everything was transcribed in my presence on my clinic notes with comments from other doctors who were doing residencies, and a nurse. Then they gave me the usual examination: blood presure, chest, temperature, etc.

I think I have certainly suffered from depression from time to time. Since yesterday, however, I am convinced that I am in full possession of my faculties. I know exactly where I am. The pit, the mud, where I thought I was, the earth worms are far away, once and for all. Mamadou did not come to see me yesterday, as I had hoped. I think he stayed with Ndeye who is certainly more ill than I am right now. I don't hold it against him any more. My vengeance once accomplished now seems useless. What a mess! Ndeye in one hospital, I in another; Awa in the other world to watch over her children.

Oumy came to see me again. She is very curious about what I am writing. I explain to her that I am trying to remember my life and that she should do the same, because it helps one to take stock of oneself. She thinks it is a waste of time, white people's business. I am going to stop writing now to go for a walk in the yard with Oumy and meet the other women.

Friday, September 8, 1961

Yesterday I did not have time to write in my diary: the whole day was filled with group activities: cooking, housework, sewing. Plus the constant coming and going of the women in the afternoon. Besides I don't seem to have anything worth writing about.

Last night, my father came to see me. He reproached me for having forgotten him and spoke to me about my mother. We went together to her tomb. It was All Souls Day and we lit a lot of candles. The whole cemetery was transformed into a sea of light. A lot of people stood near the vaults. My attention was attracted by an abandoned tomb, overgrown with grass. I pulled up a few tufts to clear a spot and lit a candle. Watching it burn, I had the impression of being inside and outside the grave at the same time. It was my tomb, there was no name on it.

This dream certainly had some deep significance which I could not grasp since it was different from my usual nightmares.

This morning after taking my shower and my medication, I went to visit some of the women in their rooms. I talked for a long time with Oumy and with Nabou who told me her story. She had gone to Paris to join her husband. When she got to France, where she could not speak French, she found herself completely cut off from the traditional family life-style of her village. Her husband was away at work all day, so she was alone, locked up, without being able to communicate with anyone. A few months later she fell ill. Her husband could not take care of her so he sent her back home and her family brought her to the hospital. She feels very well now but she doesn't want to go back to France. She wants her husband to come back so that they can go back to live in their village.

Nabou's experience in Paris strangely parallels my life in this country. We both knew the loneliness of being the 'foreigner' who had nothing to do but turn over memories for days on end, who had only one voice to listen to, her own, until it became an obsession ...

8.00 p.m.

Aunt Khady came to see me a little while ago, about six o'clock. What she told me has upset me a lot. Had I, in spite of everything, clung to a vague hope that I would win back Mamadou's affection and esteem? I realise now that I wanted to see him suffer but I had never consciously thought of his death: his eyes are closed to the light of this world, he has set off on the final journey, on the road to the village. That was where he was going last Sunday, very late at night, after he had brought me here. He lost control of his old car, which struck a tree and caught fire.

I feel drained. I have no one to love, no one to hate. I can put the final period to this diary which Mamadou will never read. I had put on mourning and cut off my hair the day I stopped living with Mamadou. For me, the world had ended on that day. Here I am today, after four years of reprieve, finally, really, all alone in the world, my heart bereft of hope. Had my life been worth living? What had I contributed, what had I given? Oh, how I long to fall asleep too, to have a long, restful night! To wake up in another world where mad people are not mad, but wise and just.

Helene had reached the end of Juletane's diary. The chanting from a neighbouring mosque signalled five o'clock. She was not sleepy. The alcohol could no longer affect her. She felt a certain melancholy. She had not known that Juletane's life had been so full of drama, and in particular that she had suffered so much. Now in her turn, she asked herself the questions which had been preoccupying her: could she have a child, at her age? Was she right to be getting married? Ousmane, of course, was nothing like Mamadou and she was the exact opposite of Juletane, but still ...

Why had she kept this notebook without having opened it? The social worker in the psychiatric services had entrusted it to her, so that she could get an idea of how much Juletane had suffered and try to find her family. She had not read it. On her return from her holidays she had phoned her colleague to tell her the results of her effort: Juletane's aunt, whom she had found, had refused to take on the responsibility of a sick niece. Helene had subsequently learnt that since her husband's death Juletane had ceased to react. She refused to eat and medication seemed to have no effect on her condition. Each day she slipped a little deeper into her dream which could only lead her to final deliverance ...

Helene tenderly smoothed the bent corners of the notebook, closed it, and, for the first time in almost twenty years, she wept. Juletane's diary had broken the block of ice around her heart.

EPILOGUE

Juletane's reprieve lasted three months after Mamadou's death. One morning the nurse on duty had found her dead. Her weary heart had simply stopped beating.

2

GLOSSARY

Beguine   French Caribbean dance

Boubou   full, loose tunic worn by men and women

Cuuraay   mixture of incense, spices and perfumes

Diriankées   courtesans

Diwunor   sort of liquid butter

Fajar   the first of five daily prayers

Griots   poet, musician, praise-singer, oral historian belonging to a special caste

Guéwé   the fifth and last prayer of the day

Kinkelibah   infusion of herbs

Maouloud   the anniversary of the birth of the prophet Mohammed

Marabout   Moslem holy man

Matoutou crabe   rice prepared with crab meat

Ounk   a sort of lizard

Pachanga   Latin American popular dance

Pagne   wrapper of loose cloth worn by both men and women

Siggil ndiggaale   to offer condolences (*Lit.* 'Bear up')

Siggil sa wall   to accept condolences with thanks

Talibés   pupils from the Koranic school

Tisbaar   the second prayer of the day, early afternoon

Toubab   a white man

Toubabesse   a white woman

THE AFRICAN AND CARIBBEAN WRITERS SERIES

The book you have been reading is part of Heinemann's long established series of African and Caribbean fiction. Details of some of the other titles available are given below, but for further information write to:
Heinemann Educational Books, 22 Bedford Square, London WC1B 3HH.

CHINUA ACHEBE
Arrow of God

A brilliantly told story of the pressures of life in the early days of white settlement. First winner of the New Statesman Jock Campbell Award.

HAROLD BASCOM
Apata

A young talented Guyanese finds the colour of his skin an insuperable barrier and is forced into a humiliating life of crime.

T. OBINKARAM ECHEWA
The Crippled Dancer

A novel of feud and intrigue set in Nigeria, by the winner of the English Speaking Union Literature Prize.

JOHN NAGENDA
The Seasons of Thomas Tebo

A pacy, vivid allegory of modern Uganda where an idyllic past stands in stark contrast to the tragic present.

NGŨGĨ WA THIONG'O
A Grain of Wheat

'With Mr Ngũgĩ, history is living tissue. He writes with poise from deep reserves, and the book adds cubits to his already considerable stature.'

The Guardian

GARTH ST OMER
The Lights on the Hill

'One of the most genuinely daring works of fiction to come my way for a very long time.'

The Listener

CHINUA ACHEBE
Things Fall Apart

Already a classic of modern writing, *Things Fall Apart* has sold well over 2,000,000 copies. 'A simple but excellent novel . . . He handles the macabre with telling restraint and the pathetic without any sense of false embarrassment.'

The Observer

ALEX LA GUMA
A Walk in the Night

Seven stories of decay, violence and poverty from the
streets of Cape Town, and by one of South Africa's most
impressive writers.

NELSON MANDELA
No Easy Walk to Freedom

A collection of the articles, speeches, letters and trials of
the most important figure in the South African liberation
struggle.

EARL LOVELACE
The Wine of Astonishment

'His writing is lyrical, reflecting Trinidadian speech habits
as well as they have ever been reflected. This is an
energetic, very unusual, above all, enlightening novel; the
author's best yet.'

Financial Times

SEMBENE OUSMANE
God's Bits of Wood

The story of a strike on the Niger–Dakar railway, by the
man who wrote and filmed *Xala*, 'Falling in the middle of
Ousmane's literary canon, before he turned to film
making, it is in some ways his most outstanding, and
certainly his most ambitious work of fiction.'

West Africa

NGŨGĨ WA THIONG'O
Petals of Blood

A compelling, passionate novel about the tragedy of corrupting power, set in post-independence Kenya.

ELECHI AMADI
Estrangement

A portrait of the aftermath of the Biafran War by one of Nigeria's leading novelists and author of *The Great Ponds*.

ZEE EDGELL
Beka Lamb

A delightful portrait of Belize, a tiny country in Central America dominated by the Catholic Church, poverty, and a matriarchal society. Winner of the Fawcett Society Book Prize.

BESSIE HEAD
A Question of Power

'She brilliantly develops ascending degrees of personal isolation, and is very moving when she describes abating pain. Her novels – and this is the third – have a way of soaring up from rock bottom to the stars, and are very shaking.'

The Sunday Times